Praise for Irene Brand and Dana Corbit's
A FAMILY FOR CHRISTMAS anthology:

"Wonderfully written, both *The Gift of Family*
and *Child in a Manger* can open up the reader's
eyes and heart to just what Christmas and
God's love really mean. Two tales that will
warm your heart this holiday season....
Make it a must-get on your present list."
—*Romance Reviews Today*

PRAISE FOR IRENE BRAND:

"Irene Brand pens a heartwarming romance
with a strong message."
—*Romantic Times*

"Ms. Brand writes stories that touch the soul
and bring the reader closer to God
with their telling...."
—*Romance Reviews Today*

On THE CHRISTMAS CHILDREN:

"...a delightful and heartwarming reminder
of the meaning of Christmas."
—*Romantic Times*

CHRISTMAS IN THE AIR

IRENE BRAND
DANA CORBIT

Steeple
Hill®

Published by Steeple Hill Books™

STEEPLE HILL BOOKS

Steeple
Hill®

ISBN 0-373-87332-8

CHRISTMAS IN THE AIR

Copyright © 2005 by Harlequin Books S.A.

The publisher acknowledges the copyright holders
of the individual works as follows:

SNOWBOUND HOLIDAY
Copyright © 2005 by Irene Brand

A SEASON OF HOPE
Copyright © 2005 by Dana Corbit Nussio

www.SteepleHill.com

Printed in U.S.A.

CONTENTS

SNOWBOUND HOLIDAY

Irene Brand

You have been a refuge for the poor, a refuge for the needy in his distress, a shelter from the storm and a shade from the heat.
—*Isaiah* 25:4

Chapter One

A thick sheet of snow and ice blanketed the interstate. Seated in the front passenger's seat of the church van, Livia Kessler's back stiffened, and she grabbed for the handle over the door every time a gust of wind swayed the vehicle sideways. Livia prayed silently for the driver, Eric Stover, who gripped the steering wheel with both hands in his attempt to control the van. She glanced over her shoulder. The other members of their church's vocal quintet slept soundly, oblivious to the dangerous weather conditions.

The singers had made their last presentation earlier in the day at a morning worship service in a large church in Detroit. They'd eaten a light lunch and started south on Interstate 75 anticipating an easy five- or six-hour drive to their destination in Columbus, Ohio.

A mixture of sleet and rain had been falling when they left Detroit, but they'd soon left the moisture behind. When they crossed Michigan's state line into Ohio, they drove a few miles without any precipitation. As they'd bypassed the city of Toledo, however, they encountered a wind-driven, wet snow that accumulated quickly on the highway.

The flip-flap-flop of the wipers as they moved rhythmically back and forth on the windshield mesmerized Livia. She started yawning. Knowing she had to stay awake to encourage Eric, she opened the window a gap to bring fresh air into the van. The air was fresh, all right. In fact, it was frigid. She hurriedly closed the window.

"If this keeps up we won't make it back to Columbus tonight," she said quietly.

Taking a deep breath, Eric said, "I know. If the snow is heading northeast, we'll soon move past it. If not, we'd better look for a motel."

Tomorrow would be Christmas Eve, and all of them wanted to get home before then. "But Sean's plane leaves for California at ten o'clock," Livia said, knowing that the tenor member of their singing group wanted to be home for Christmas.

Nodding his head, Eric said, "I know, but I'm more concerned about our safety than his plane trip. When a strong wind gust sideswipes the van, I don't have much control over it. Can you turn on the radio? It may wake the others, but I'd like to hear a weather report."

Livia scanned the radio options until she picked up a strong FM station. They'd just missed the news apparently, because the DJ said, "Folks, sit back and listen to your favorite Christmas songs."

The gentle sounds of "I'll Be Home for Christmas" increased Livia's disappointment. Sean wasn't the only one who wanted to go home. Livia was a student at Ohio State University, and she intended to leave for her home in southern Ohio as soon as they returned from the singing engagement. In her twenty years, she had never missed a Christmas on Heritage Farm. If they had to lay over at a motel until this storm was over, she wouldn't make it home to observe Christmas with her parents, siblings and her little nephew. She couldn't miss Derek's first Christmas!

Eric slowed when they reached the city limits of Bowling Green. The change of pace awakened the passengers. Tall, thin Sean King unfolded his muscular legs, rubbed his eyes and leaned forward as a meteorologist announced, "We interrupt our musical program for a severe weather warning. A blizzard, with wind gusts in excess of forty miles per hour, is sweeping across northwestern Ohio. In some areas, a foot of snow already covers the ground, with a predicted accumulation of another foot or more in the next twenty-four hours. Stay off the highways unless it's an emergency."

"You should have gotten me up," Sean said. "Do you want me to drive for a while, Eric?"

"Yes, I'd appreciate some help," Eric said. "Visibility is poor, and I've been fighting this side wind for so long, my muscles are tied in knots. As soon as I find a place to pull over, you can drive."

Marie, Eric's wife, sat up and rubbed her husband's

tense shoulders. "Oh, I didn't realize it was snowing like this. I should have stayed awake."

"You couldn't have done anything, honey, and you were sleeping so soundly that I don't want to wake you," Eric explained.

"Will we make it home tonight?" Marie asked, voicing the major concern of all of them.

"I doubt it, unless we run out of the storm soon," Eric said. "I hope you don't miss your plane, Sean."

"Hey, man, don't worry about that," Sean said. "Depending on the direction of the storm, the Columbus airport may be closed anyway. Don't take any risks for my sake. How long before we come to another town?"

Livia took a map out of the glove compartment, and turned on the interior light. In the small ray of light, she scanned the map. "It's several miles to Findlay. We should find a motel there, but there's no town of any size before then. And if you remember from our drive on this road a few days ago, after we leave Findlay, it's mostly rural area until we approach Columbus. So that means no motels. We can't go farther than Findlay."

Livia relaxed when a highway marker indicated the next exit was two miles away. "Maybe we can find a motel at this exit," she said.

"Well, even if we don't, I'm getting off the interstate, so we can change drivers," Eric said.

But through the haze of snow, in the distance, Livia saw lights flashing. "Oh, no!" she said. "Looks like a police cruiser. There's probably been a wreck."

Eric slowed to a crawl, but the car still skidded

sideways when he applied the brakes and missed hitting the patrol car by inches. An officer, bracing himself against the strong wind, held on to his hat as he approached the van.

"A pileup of vehicles has blocked the interstate between here and the next exit," the officer said. "You'll have to get off and take a secondary road south. You can access the interstate again in twelve miles. Be careful—it's a narrow road."

"Any chance we can find a motel, Officer?" Livia said.

"Not till you get to Findlay."

Another car approached behind them, and the patrolman waved them on.

"I'll keep driving, Sean. With all this snow, I can't tell where to pull off the highway." Eric wiggled back and forth in the seat and flexed his fingers before he moved forward. "Hindsight is better than foresight, I've always heard," he said. "We should have stayed overnight in Bowling Green."

Livia had been checking the outdoor thermometer on the dashboard, which registered steadily falling temperatures. Now, rather than being distressed about not getting home for Christmas, she prayed that they could find a safe shelter for the night. She'd learned the seriousness of blizzards a few years ago when a heavy snow, accompanied by an ice storm, immobilized their farm in southern Ohio. That had been Christmas week, too—the time her brother, Evan, had brought his fiancée home to spend the holidays with the family.

The headlights of the van were little help in the blinding snow, and Eric dodged twice to keep from hitting approaching vehicles on the narrow road. A large panel truck crept along the road in front of them, and Eric stayed close behind it.

"I have no sense of direction right now, but I figure that guy knows where he's going," he explained. "I'll keep him in sight."

The truck slowed to a crawl at a crossroad. The snow had covered the highway direction signs, but when the truck continued straight ahead, Eric followed. This section of road was even more narrow than the one they'd taken when they left the interstate. Fence posts and bushes covered with snow had turned the road into a narrow tunnel, and Livia couldn't see any houses or farm buildings at all. The van's bumper pushed a wall of snow ahead of it as they moved steadily forward.

Darkness had almost fallen when, with sinking heart, Livia saw the truck swerve to one side and slide into a ditch. When the driver attempted to pull out of the slide, the truck jackknifed across the road.

Livia's plummeting heart echoed Sean's words when he predicted, "It will take a wrecker to right that truck."

Gingerly applying the brakes of the van, Eric said, "Let's find out if the driver is injured."

Before Eric brought the van to a sliding halt, the truck driver climbed out of the cab, seemingly none the worse for his accident.

Knowing that they couldn't go forward, Livia rolled down her window and looked behind them to see if they could turn and retrace their route. A pickup truck and a car were following them. The driver of the pickup braked to avoid hitting the van. The old sedan behind the pickup swerved quickly to the side of the road to avoid rear-ending the pickup. The car slid sideways and stalled in a large drift, blocking the road.

"We can't go either way now," Livia said, desperation in her voice. A chilly silence enveloped the van.

Livia snatched her cell phone from her bag. A tight knot filled her throat when she saw that no service was available in this area.

"We can't use our phones, either," she said, a tremor in her voice.

Roxanne Fisher, Marie's mother, peered out the window and said, "So we're stranded."

Eric rolled down the window, stuck his head out and called to the other three travelers, who were circling their own vehicles, sizing up the situation.

"Hey, guys! Looks like we're all stuck. Get in our van, and we'll discuss our options."

Sean moved to the rear seat, sat beside Roxanne and made space for the newcomers. The three men were covered with snow when they stepped into the van. Livia gasped when the ceiling light illuminated the face of one of the men.

Quinn Damron! She turned away so he couldn't see her face. The situation was already difficult enough without encountering *this* man. Especially a man whose rejection three years ago had left her heart empty and injured—a heart that had never found room for another.

Livia stared out the side window as she listened to the conversation, hoping no one had noticed her reaction and would ask her about it later.

"Any of you familiar with this area?" Eric asked. "Is there any chance of finding shelter for the night?"

One of the men, a senior citizen, said, "Yes, sir. I've lived around here nigh on to eighty years. There ain't a house in five miles of where we are."

"Any chance of getting plowed out?" the truck driver asked.

"Not until it stops snowing. I'd judge it'll be two to three days before we get any help. The snowplows will clear the interstates and major highways before they get to us. How'd you end up here anyway? This road ain't hardly ever used."

"I apparently took a wrong turn," the truck driver admitted. "I haven't made deliveries on this road before. The regular driver is on vacation. The snow had covered the road signs, and after we took several turns on that little road from the interstate, I lost my sense of direction. So I took a chance on which way to go and my luck didn't hold."

"I'm not familiar with this country, either," Eric said. "I decided this was the detour route when the truck came this way."

"Sorry I led you astray, buddy," the trucker said.

"You're no more to blame than we are," Eric assured him.

"We probably shouldn't leave the cars to find shelter," Quinn said. Livia's pulse raced at the mellow, deep voice that she still vividly recalled, erasing any doubt that he was the unforgettable man she'd met three years ago.

"And it's going to be miserable sleeping in them," Sean said.

"Especially since the temperature is supposed to drop below zero tomorrow," Quinn agreed. "I'm only twenty-five miles from home, but it might as well be a hundred miles for all the good it will do me."

"Livia," Eric said, "lower the window and try your cell phone again."

Did she hear a quick intake of breath from Quinn's direction? He'd known her as "Olivia," and there was certainly other women named Olivia out there, so it was probably her imagination. Without answering, she lowered the window, and held her phone out. But the screen still showed that she had no service. They were probably too far away for her to get a signal, and the storm certainly wasn't helping any. She shook her head at Eric, not wanting to speak, fearing that Quinn would recognize her voice. But knowing the little interest that he'd had in her, she thought bitterly, he probably hadn't given her a second thought since the last time they'd seen each other.

The elderly gentleman said, "My name's Les Holden. Since I've been around a few years longer than the rest of you, I feel free to offer some suggestions. I've lived through blizzards in this area before, and if the snow drifts, these cars could be covered. Besides, even if you wrap up, you're gonna get cold in the van."

"I think all of us know that," Sean said impatiently, "but what else can we do?"

Favoring Sean with an amused glance from under his shaggy white eyebrows, Les said, "Hold your horses, sonny, I'm coming to that." He waved his hand in the direction of the panel truck. "I almost forget. There's an abandoned church down the road a short ways, and I think we oughta move down there before it gets any darker."

"But if it's abandoned, it won't be any warmer than the cars," Sean argued. "If we stay here, we can start the motor once in a while and run the heater."

"Not if the snow gets so deep it covers our exhaust pipes," Quinn said quietly.

"There ain't been regular services in this church for years," Les continued, as if the other two hadn't spoken, "but the building is still in good shape. We use it every once in a while for funerals, so there's coal and wood on hand to build fires. We can keep a fire going. We're apt to be stranded for a day or two, so we'll be more comfortable and safer in the church than in our vehicles."

"I agree with you," Quinn said. "What do the rest of you think?"

"Wonder if there's any food in the church?" Sean said. "I'm hungry now, and fasting for a few days doesn't sound good to me."

"You'll be hungry no matter where you are," Les said shortly.

"I can help out there," the truck driver said. "My

truck is full of groceries. We can take food out of it and pay my boss for whatever we use."

Marie and Roxanne voiced their approval of Les's plan, and it seemed the general consensus that they must move to the church. Apparently aware that she hadn't said anything, Eric said, "Is that all right with you, Livia?"

In a quiet voice, she said, "It's the only thing we can do. I've experienced enough snowstorms and power outages on our farm to know it's going to be unpleasant no matter where we are."

"Then if everyone agrees, you take charge, Les," Quinn said. "You're more experienced in this sort of thing than we are. Lead on to the church."

Quinn peered intently at the back of Livia's head. Could this be the Olivia Kessler he'd known at one time? Her voice sounded familiar, and she did live in Ohio, but it had been a few years. If this was the woman he'd known, and the two of them were destined to spend several days in the same building, the atmosphere might be decidedly tense. But despite the awkwardness of the past, Quinn hadn't forgotten her. He looked forward to renewing their friendship, but he wasn't proud of his past actions. He opened the car door and stepped out into the falling snow. How forgiving would Olivia be to him for breaking her heart?

Chapter Two

Quinn recalled Olivia Kessler had straight, blond hair that fell below her shoulders, just as this woman did. She'd been a tall, willowy young woman, quick and graceful. The focal point of the gentle beauty of her face had been her deep blue eyes fringed by long lashes. He wished he could get a better look at her, but this Livia woman hadn't once turned so he could see her features.

"We might have to make more'n one trip," Les said as he ducked his head against the cold wind. Quinn put thoughts of the past aside and devoted his attention to the man's instructions.

"Take everything you can the first time. Wear your heaviest coats and take blankets if you have any. Let's go single file, and keep one hand free to hold on to the person in front of you. It's easy to get separated in a blizzard. Those of you in the van, wait here until the rest of us gather what we can from our vehicles."

Livia exchanged her sneakers for fleece-lined boots and laced them securely. She shrugged into a heavy coat as she recalled the four weeks she'd spent with Quinn at a 4-H camp in eastern Ohio. She'd gone as a volunteer worker, and she'd been assigned to work with Quinn, the camp counselor.

Eight years her senior, he had been the perfect man of her dreams. They'd been together for hours every day, and Livia had developed a huge crush on him. Because of his kindness and attentiveness to her, she thought he shared her feelings. She'd been too naive to see that he treated everyone in the same friendly way. A few times, she had even imagined that he wanted to kiss her. When he didn't, she reasoned that Quinn considered it inappropriate to make any advances when they were supervising the younger campers. She'd dreamed that their relationship would deepen when they were no longer working at the camp.

The last night of the camp, she'd given Quinn an impassioned letter, the memory of which still made her face burn. She hadn't said she loved him, but she didn't hide her obvious feelings for him, writing that she didn't want him to go out of her life.

Quinn left the camp early the next morning without saying goodbye or acknowledging the note. This rejection left her feeling foolish and hurt. Livia hadn't forgotten him, however, and she'd often wondered if her infatuation for Quinn *had* been real love. She'd never found any other man to interest her. Still smarting from Quinn's rejection, she dreaded being confined with him for days.

Livia tied the hood of her fleece-lined coat below her chin. She placed her Bible, a historical novel, a notebook, a pen and a bag of trail mix in a large tote bag, which she slung over her shoulder. She carried a small garment bag in her right hand. The wind staggered her when she stepped out, and she held to the side of the van as she joined the others.

Sean was visibly shivering. A resident of southern California, he had come to OSU four years ago on a basketball scholarship. He liked the school, but had never adjusted to the climate, which differed so much from his childhood home. Regardless of how many heavy winter clothes he put on, he was always miserable when cold weather struck Ohio.

Looking like a bunch of pack animals, they huddled together in the shelter of the van until Les and the other men joined them.

"I'll go first," Les said. He pointed to Roxanne Fisher. "You fall in behind me, ma'am, and the rest of you line up behind us. Don't worry about looking forward to where you're going. I'll be your guide. Keep your eyes on the ground, follow my steps and hold on to the person in front of you."

Eric stepped into line behind his mother-in-law, and Marie stood behind him. Quinn moved behind Marie, and Sean motioned for Livia to go ahead of him. She didn't want to touch Quinn, and she had no choice but to follow him. Quinn had a large pack over his shoulder, and he carried a snow shovel in his left hand.

Sean placed a trembling hand on Livia's shoulder.

She felt sorry for the guy. He was a great basketball player; he just couldn't cope with the cold and snow. Peering over her shoulder, Livia saw the truck driver take up the rear.

Above the whine of the wind, Les shouted, "Everybody ready?" Livia marveled at his foghorn voice, unusual for a man of his age. "Tug on the person in front of you, so I'll know you're in line."

When Sean squeezed Livia's shoulder, she tugged on the sleeve of Quinn's coat. It would have been simpler to tap him on the shoulder, because he was only a few inches taller than she was, but Livia couldn't bear the thought of any personal contact with Quinn.

The foolishness of her crush on Quinn had been a heavy weight on her heart for three years. How could she endure the embarrassment of facing him again?

As she trudged along in Quinn's wake, to take her mind off this man who so suddenly had come into her life again, Livia thought of Heritage Farm and her family. Christmas observance was important to the Kesslers, and she knew that, short of a sudden ninety-degree heat wave, she couldn't possibly be home for Christmas. Probably right now, her mother would be preparing the stollen, a traditional bread recipe that her ancestors had brought from Germany. Her brother Evan would have already brought the live Christmas tree into their large living room for decorating. Uncle Gavin and his wife, Emmalee, would have arrived from Florida.

Quinn stopped abruptly. Livia stumbled forward, her face landing in the middle of his back.

"We must be at the church," he said.

His words were welcome to Livia, because although they'd walked only a short distance, her face was numb from exposure to the wind-driven snow. Inside her lightweight gloves, Livia's fingers tingled with cold.

Shielding her eyes against the icy snow, Livia saw a gray, weather-beaten frame church. Three steps led to a small porch that sheltered the front door, over which a sign was nailed, indicating that Sheltering Arms Church had been established in 1901. The church would live up to its name tonight by providing safety for eight stranded travelers. For the first time, Livia wondered if God had a reason for bringing all of them together.

Les stood in front of the door, fumbling in his pocket. Drawing out a chain holding several keys, he chose one, inserted it in the lock and pushed the door inward. He peered inside, then motioned his companions to follow him. Quinn stood aside for Livia to proceed him into the building. She nodded her thanks.

The inside of the structure was dark and uninviting. For a few moments, it seemed warm because the fierce wind and the snow-and-ice mixture were no longer stinging Livia's face. As her eyes adjusted to the dim interior, Livia noted that the building was small and neglected, although it must have been a beautiful sanctuary in its day.

The front wall of the church held a stained-glass window depicting Jesus as the Good Shepherd. The six other windows, three on each side of the church, had frosted panes. A dark wainscoting covered the lower half of the walls. Faded wallpaper reached from the wainscoting to the ceiling.

An old-fashioned pump organ was located to one side of the room with an upright piano beside it. An ornately carved wooden lectern was centered on a raised platform below the decorative window. A stove stood in the middle of the room, with a rusty stovepipe sticking through the ceiling. About twenty wooden pews completed the room's furnishings.

With a speculative glance around the room, Quinn said, "We couldn't expect any better accommodations than this under the circumstances. You said there's wood and coal available, right?" he asked Les.

"Yeah, stored in a building back of the church. There are some shovels in the supply room by the back door. We still dig graves by hand, and we keep the shovels for that. They'll come in handy for scooping coal and snow. We can shovel a path to the woodshed and carry in fuel to get the fire started."

Quinn lifted his own shovel. "I always carry a snow shovel in the truck this time of year. If the two of us can take care of scooping away the snow and bringing in the coal and wood, perhaps you other men can bring supplies from the delivery truck. It's getting dark fast."

When the other men agreed, Les said, "Just bring enough food and water to keep us through the night. Maybe the storm will run its course by morning, and we can shovel our way to our vehicles for whatever we need."

Pushing back the hood of her coat, Livia asked, "What can I do?"

"Look in the supply room for candles and holders," Les answered. He called to the men, who were leaving, "If you have any extra flashlights in your vehicles, bring them along."

Quinn took the scarf from his neck and wound it around his head to secure his cap. Pulling on woolen mittens, he followed Les out the back door. Not wasting any time, Les started shoveling. Bracing himself against the strong wind, Quinn stepped to Les's side. He'd grown up on a farm in this area, and more than once, he'd helped clear deep snow from around the farm buildings. He'd volunteered for this task, because he figured the other men hadn't had as much experience in rough living as he'd had.

Livia still hadn't made any indication that she recognized him, but he didn't doubt at all that she was the Olivia he'd met at a camp a few years ago. He had harbored some romantic thoughts of her until he'd learned that she was still in her late teens, while he was twenty-five. In addition to that problem, he still had two more years before he would receive his veterinarian's license. His busy school schedule left no time for romance. He'd shied away from dating a high school girl, but he'd often wondered if he'd made a mistake in not keeping in touch with Olivia.

Believing firmly that God intervened in the lives of His followers, Quinn thought this might not be a chance encounter. Could God have a purpose in a reunion between Olivia and himself?

It was difficult to clear the path because of the steadily falling snow. Their tracks were covered almost as soon as they moved onward. Quinn stopped, straightened, and took a deep breath.

"Pace yourself," Les shouted above the fury of the wind. "Don't overdo."

Quinn nodded his understanding. The woodshed stood only thirty feet from the church, but his body was practically steaming when they reached the building. Stepping inside, he helped Les fill three large buckets with coal and sticks of wood.

Breathing deeply, Les said, "Which do you want to do, carry the coal inside and start a fire, or clean a path to the johnny houses?"

As he'd been shoveling, Quinn had noticed the two wooden toilets a few feet beyond the woodshed. Since the church had been abandoned for a long time, he'd figured there wouldn't be any usable inside plumbing to make life easier for them.

"I'll shovel," he said. "I haven't built a fire in a stove for a long time. You'll be better at it. Take two of the buckets. I'll bring the third one and the shovels when I finish clearing the paths."

The search of the supply room yielded about a dozen used candles and several holders, which the women placed around the room.

Marie, who wasn't often disturbed by difficult circumstances, assessed their accommodations. Laughing lightly, she said, "I can't decide which will be the most comfortable for sleeping—the floor or the wooden pews."

Marie's mother, Roxanne, who always described herself as pleasingly plump, said, "I'll opt for the floor. There's no room for me on a pew."

Les struggled into the church, carrying two buckets of fuel and shouted, "Will one of you ladies close the door behind me?"

Marie rushed to the door and strained to shut it against the force of the wind. Livia added her strength to Marie's and they slammed the door, but a thin sheet of snow slithered across the floor before they had finished. Livia brought a rag from the supply room and mopped up the snow before it froze on the cold floor.

Les removed his gloves and blew on his hands to warm them. When he opened the door of the stove, Livia said, "I'll start the fire for you."

Les lifted his shaggy brows in surprise. "You know how to lay a fire, ma'am?"

"Sure do," Livia said. "We have a big fireplace in the living room of our farmhouse. We always have a fire in the evening during the winter. I learned to start a fire when I was just a kid."

Les watched with interest as she adjusted the draft on the stovepipe and sifted the ashes from the last fire into the ash pan. She picked up some small sticks of wood from a nearby box filled with wood and paper and arranged the kindling loosely in the stove.

"Since the church isn't used anymore, is the flue

safe?" she asked. "We could have some heat we don't want if the ceiling catches on fire."

"I clean the chimney every fall, just to be sure a bird hasn't nested in it, or to see if any bricks might have crumbled and caused a blockage. It's all right."

Livia took a newspaper from the box and pushed it in around the kindling. "I'm hoping one of the men has matches or a lighter we can use."

"There's matches here," Les said. He walked into the supply room and came back with a Mason jar full of matches. "If I didn't keep the matches covered, a mouse might chew into one of them and start a fire," he explained.

"Oh, I've heard of church mice," Marie said, laughing, "or at least about people who were poor as church mice. That's our situation tonight."

"We won't be bothered with mice," Les assured her with a sly grin. "I'd judge that they've buried deep in the ground to get out of the snow."

Roxanne took several matches. "I'll light the candles."

Livia struck a match on the side of the stove and held it to the paper. She watched carefully as the paper blazed and spread to the slivers of wood. When she adjusted the damper to control the blaze, Les said approvingly, "That's a good job, miss. Let me take over now and put the coal on the fire—no need for you to dirty your hands."

Quinn smelled the smoke before he finished shoveling the paths to the "necessaries," as the pioneers had called them. He even sensed some warmth from the stove when he went inside the church.

"Come close to the stove," Les said, "and warm yourself. You had a cold job."

Quinn shivered involuntarily. "It must be zero by now." Glancing around, he saw that the men hadn't returned from the truck. "I'll go help the others with the food and supplies in a minute, after I warm up a bit."

Livia remembered that Quinn had always pulled more than his share of the load at the 4-H camp. He apparently hadn't changed.

Les cracked the front door of the church and peered out. "With that truck over on its side, I figure they had a hard time getting into it. But I hear them coming now."

He held the door open for the men to enter. On the porch, they shook themselves like dogs to remove the snow from their clothes.

"Brrr!" Sean said. "If I ever get home to California, I'm never coming east again."

"Oh, you'll forget that after your next basketball game," Eric said. "Although I'll admit this is miserable weather, and I'd welcome some California sunshine myself."

Marie helped her husband unwrap the scarf from around his head. "Did you bring any food? I'm hungry."

"We did," Sean grumbled, "but it wasn't easy. There's almost two feet of snow already and it's still falling."

As the others made room for the three men to hover

around the stove, Eric looked around the candlelit room. "It seems peaceful in here," he said. "If we had to be stranded, we could be in worse places. God made provisions for us—a dry, warm place to stay and a truck full of food."

"I'll have to keep a list of what we brought," the truck driver said, "so we can offer to pay for the supplies. But under the circumstances, I don't think the boss will charge us for what we use."

They rearranged three of the pews to circle the stove, where they crowded close together for body warmth and to eat their evening meal. Cheese, crackers, apples and cookies seemed like a banquet to a starving Livia. The men had brought several cartons of bottled water and soft drinks to supplement the meal.

Before they started to eat, Eric asked the blessing for the food and thanked God for their safety. For once, Livia couldn't be thankful for what God had given her. She was miserable. Not only did she want to be with her family, she definitely didn't want to be thrown into Quinn's company. Livia swiped away her tears. If she started crying, it would tear down the fragile defenses of the others, who were trying to make the best of a bad situation.

Livia's parents had always taught their children that God orchestrated every facet of their lives, but tonight, Livia found that hard to accept.

God, if I had to be stranded, why did Quinn Damron have to be here, too?

Chapter Three

When they finished eating, Eric said, "I firmly believe that God rules in the destiny of His creation, and for some reason, He brought us together tonight. I don't know what it is yet, and we may never know, but I suggest we accept the situation and move on. It's going to be a long night. Let's introduce ourselves, so we can at least call each other by name, instead of saying, 'Hey, you.'"

"Sounds good," Quinn said. "I'll start."

Warmth radiated from the stove now, and in the subdued light of the candles, it could have been a peaceful setting except for the dangerous conditions lurking outside the building.

The screeching wind rattled the windows and forced an occasional puff of smoke back down the chimney. Drifting snow sifted in around the doors, as if warning the travelers of potential disaster looming a few steps away.

Quinn sat directly across the circle from Livia, and she kept her eyes downcast as he talked. She hadn't yet looked directly at him. She knew she'd have to face up to her embarrassing past sometime and go on with her life. Perhaps tonight was the time.

Quinn unbuttoned the heavy coat he wore, since the room was getting warm. "My name is Quinn Damron. I'm in partnership with my father on a horse farm located about twenty-five miles from here. I'm also a farrier. Does anyone know what that is?"

Livia knew, but she didn't want to call attention to herself.

"I know," Les said. "He shoes horses."

"That's true, and some, like myself, also treat animals' diseases. I'm a licensed veterinarian, but I decided to work on the farm a year or so before I set up my practice."

"Married?" Eric inquired.

Quinn squirmed uncomfortably. "Not yet," he said. He'd been dating a neighbor for a year, but for some reason, he couldn't get serious about marrying her.

"Who's next?" Eric prodded.

The truck driver sitting to Quinn's left, said, "Might as well be me, I guess. My name's Allen Reynolds. I'm thirty, married, with two cute little daughters. I intended to be home tonight to help them trim the Christmas tree." His voice faltered, and he dropped his head, apparently unable to say more.

It was Sean's turn, and he said, "I'm sorry I've been so grumpy, but I feel better now that I'm getting warm.

I'm Sean King, and I expected to go home to California tonight. After hearing about Allen's kids, I don't have any complaint, but I may complain anyway," he added with a fetching grin. "I guess that's enough about me."

"I don't think so," Roxanne Fisher said, her brown eyes shimmering in the dim light as she introduced herself. "Sean is a senior at the university, and this will be his fourth season to play basketball at OSU. You'll probably see him on national television playing in the NBA in a year or two. Besides that, he's a member of our church, and the tenor member of our quintet."

"Hey, Roxanne," Sean objected. "You're supposed to be talking about *yourself*."

"Which I will do now," the vivacious woman said, laughing. "I'm the music director at the Westside Community Church in Columbus. Sean, Marie, Eric and Livia are members of the church's quintet. I play the piano for the others to sing. In fact, we're returning from Detroit where we sang at the home church of one of our quintet members. We left him with his family for the holidays."

As Roxanne talked, Livia realized she would be next, and she didn't know what to say. If Quinn hadn't recognized her by now, he probably would when she mentioned her family. But on the other hand, he may have completely forgotten the personal information he'd learned in the four weeks they'd worked together. Obviously it hadn't meant much to him, or he would have answered her letter.

Roxanne nudged her, and Livia realized she'd been lost in thought. "I'm Olivia Kessler, but my friends call me Livia. I live on a farm in southern Ohio, near the city of Gallipolis. I'm in my sophomore year at OSU." Her brief comments confirmed Quinn's belief that she was the young woman he had met a few years ago. He tried to catch her eye to acknowledge their former acquaintance, but without looking at him, Livia waved a hand to Eric, indicating that she'd finished.

"I'm the youth minister at Westside," Eric introduced himself. "I'm also working on my master's degree in theology."

Livia knew Eric so well that she didn't have to listen to his introduction. Her mind wandered again as she glanced around the room, thinking what a diverse group they were, not only in occupations and family background, but also in looks. Quinn had chestnut-brown hair, high cheekbones, a strong chin and a firm mouth. His long-limbed body was closer to six feet tall, and he was broad-shouldered. She couldn't see his eyes in the semidarkness, but she remembered that they were a vivid green.

Sean's eyes were a deep shade of brown, and he had light brown hair. Several inches over six feet, he moved with the easy stride of an athlete.

Allen Reynolds, a tall, massive man, was muscular rather than fat. His hair was black, and in the shadows, his dark eyes gleamed from deep orbs.

Marie Stover and her mother, Roxanne, looked alike. Both had brown hair and eyes, and their dusky, round oval faces bordered on perfection. Marie was twenty-eight, and Roxanne had been twenty when her only child was born. It was only in personality that their differences were obvious. Marie was laid-back and amiable, while Roxanne possessed a dynamic, sometimes aggressive, personality—attributes that had made her effective as the director of the musical program in a large church.

Eric was a tall, thin man who appeared frail. However, none of the teenagers he counseled could keep up with his zeal and enthusiasm in the sports and work projects he initiated.

When Les Holden started to speak, Livia gave him her undivided attention. She already appreciated the man because he'd guided them to the security of this church. Les wasn't more than five feet tall, obviously suffering with arthritis, although he wouldn't have been a big man even in his youth. Partly bald, he had a fringe of gray hair that matched the bushy gray eyebrows that extended like shingles over his faded blue eyes.

"I ain't much for making speeches," he said. "Like I told you, I'll be eighty my next birthday. I've been a widower for twenty-some years. I know how quick these storms can come, and I shouldn't have started out tonight. I aimed to spend Christmas with my daughter, who lives about ten miles away. But she won't worry when I don't show up, thinking that I'm still safe at home. That's about all, I guess."

"Les, why isn't the church used anymore?" Livia asked. "I'm grateful for its sheltering walls tonight, and it seems sad that this building is no longer a light-house for God in this community."

"Yes'um, I agree with you." He stood stiffly and walked around, apparently to exercise his arthritic limbs. "I remember comin' here with Mom and Dad when I was a young'un. This room would be crowded every Sunday. We sure enjoyed praising the Lord within these walls."

"If I remember right," Quinn said, "there used to be a town in this area."

"Yes, sir, that's right. The town of Bexter was built in the late 1800s. There was a railroad here, running between Akron and Chicago. Probably as many as five hundred people lived here once, but after World War II, a lot of railroad lines consolidated and little railways were shut down. The loss of the railroad killed the town. People started moving away, and finally there weren't enough left to keep the church going. A lot of my kin-folk are buried in the cemetery across the road, and some of my neighbors asked me to keep up the building and grounds. Not much else I can do anymore."

"Tell us about the stained-glass window," Marie said. "It doesn't fit with the plain architecture of the rest of the building."

"This town was named for a railroad man, Addison Bexter. He donated the window as a memorial to his parents. Because of the way Jesus is cradling the lamb in His arms, the members called their meeting house the Sheltering Arms Church. There's a little plaque on the window—you can read it in the morning."

While Les had talked, Marie had leaned her head on Eric's shoulder. When she yawned noisily, Eric laughed and said, "I think my wife is ready for bed, such as it is."

Favoring his stiff knees, Les peered out the window. "It's almost stopped snowing, but the wind's still gusty."

Quinn peered over Les's shoulder. "Looks like a good two feet of snow, wouldn't you say?"

"At least that much," Les agreed. "It's let up, but there's bound to be some drifting."

As if to reinforce his words, a gust of wind rattled the windowpanes. The gust gave way to a shrill screech that whirled around the church, making goose bumps break out on Livia's body.

"The rest of you get what sleep you can," Les said. "I'll stay up and keep the fire going. It's kinda cozy in here now, but when the temperature drops outside, it'll get colder."

"It isn't fair for you to shoulder all the responsibility," Livia objected. "I know how to stoke a fire. We're in this together. I'll take my turn."

"So will I," Quinn said.

When all of the castaways insisted that they wanted to help out, Eric said, "Let's divide into four groups of two and keep watch." He looked at his watch. "It's nine o'clock now, and it won't be daylight until seven. That's ten hours, which we can divide into two-and-a-half-hour segments. Even if she is sleepy, Marie and I will take the first shift."

"I'll watch with Sean," Roxanne said, with a fond glance at the basketball star. "I'll keep him awake."

Les looked at the truck driver. "We'd probably make a good team," he said. Allen nodded his agreement.

"Then that leaves Olivia and me," Quinn said, and experienced a quickening of his heartbeat. He darted a questioning glance at her. "Is that okay?"

It definitely wasn't okay, but what could she say? How could she spend over two hours with a man for whom she'd harbored bitter thoughts for three years? She'd finally gotten to the point where she'd put her crush on Quinn behind her. Why had he entered her life again?

Unwilling to allow him to think that his presence bothered her, she met his eyes directly for the first time. "Of course," she said.

Perhaps these solitary hours with Quinn would erase her bitter memories and pave the way so they could become friends again.

With twenty pews at their disposal, preparations for bed were simple. They'd gathered several blankets from their vehicles, so the people who were sleeping, or trying to, could each have a covering. As cold as the room was when they moved a few feet from the stove, no one considered removing their bulky outerwear.

Since the snow had accumulated several more inches, Quinn and Allen cleared the paths to the woodshed and the johnny houses again. Eric and Les carried in more fuel to last through the night.

The trip to the outside necessary was an experience Livia would never forget. Life on the farm, and summer camping events, had prepared her for rough living, but nothing she'd experienced could prepare her for this jaunt when the wind was blowing forty miles per hour and the snow was two feet deep.

Hustling toward the necessary, Livia felt like she was in a tunnel, because the shoveled snow was heaped high on both sides of the path. The tunnel provided plenty of privacy, and Roxanne carried a large battery-driven spotlight that Quinn had brought from his truck. Despite their discomfort and unfamiliarity with this rugged substitute for plumbing, Marie and Roxanne, teeth chattering, giggled about the experience as they waited their turn in the one-person accommodation.

When all eight of them were back in the church building, Quinn warned, "Don't anyone go out alone tonight for any reason. If someone slips and falls, without any help, it could be fatal."

Preparing for the first watch, Eric and Marie cuddled under a blanket on a pew close to the stove. Livia extinguished all of the candles except two. Since they didn't know how long they'd be snowbound, they needed to conserve their small stock of candles.

Quinn and Livia were scheduled for the two o'clock shift.

Worried about being away from home and frustrated over this chance meeting with Quinn, Livia wondered if she would get any rest. Unwelcome thoughts scampered wildly through her mind. She knew that she was in for a long night of soul-searching.

Sitting on a front pew, Livia focused her attention on the stained-glass window, barely visible in the dim light. It was her custom to read the Bible and pray before she went to sleep at night. Since there wasn't enough light for her to read, she was thankful for the Scriptures that she'd memorized. Inspired by the picture of Jesus holding a lamb in His arms, she remembered the Twenty-Third Psalm, which she'd learned as a child.

"'The Lord is my Shepherd I shall not want,'" she whispered, and meditated on the rest of the psalm. She repeated quietly the verse that seemed to be the most pertinent tonight.

"'Yea, though I walk through the valley of the shadow of death, I will fear no evil: for Thou art with me; Thy rod and Thy staff they comfort me.'"

Perhaps at no other time in her life had it been necessary for her to put this promise to the test. Her life up until now had been relatively carefree. Except for her secret liking for Quinn, never before had Livia encountered any crisis when she didn't have her family to lean on.

Fortunately, their lives weren't at risk, but their situation would have been dire if God hadn't directed them along this isolated road to the Sheltering Arms Church. If they'd stayed on the interstate, they might easily have been in a deadly accident. Livia believed when anyone was wholly committed to the will of God,

He directed that person's daily walk. In spite of her sorrow at missing Christmas with her family, Livia's uneasiness lessened. Whatever His reason, she believed that she was in the place God wanted her to be tonight.

Kneeling, Livia rested her head on the pew, finding comfort in being in a place where people had worshiped long ago.

God, thanks for Your protection on this stormy night. I pray that You will give my parents peace of mind. I know they are worried about me. I'm thankful for this opportunity to witness Your love and goodness with my dear friends, and the ones I've met tonight for the first time. And about Quinn, Lord? When no other man has ever been able to replace him in my heart, does that mean he's the one You've meant for me all along? Is that the reason we're snowbound? Whatever the outcome, Lord, I praise You for Your watchful eye, yesterday, today and forever. Amen.

Livia was warm enough in her heavy clothes, so instead of wrapping in the blanket, she folded it under her head as a pillow. She didn't remove her boots when she stretched out on the hard pew. She wasn't a large person, but the only way she found any comfort was by turning on her left side and curling up in a fetal position. Sleepily, she wondered how anyone the size of Quinn or Allen Reynolds could find rest on these narrow benches.

Livia felt as if she'd just gone to sleep when Quinn touched her shoulder. Stiff from lying on the wooden bench, and tense from drifting in and out of sleep for the past several hours, Livia could hardly move. She struggled to a sitting position, rubbed her eyes and moved quietly to sit on the bench beside the stove, which Les and Allen were now vacating.

Les opened the door of the stove and laid several chunks of coal and two sticks of wood on a glowing bed of coals. "You probably won't have to do anything for an hour," he whispered.

"We'll be fine," Livia assured him, keeping her voice low so that she wouldn't disturb anyone who was sleeping. "You rest and don't worry about us."

Livia propped her feet on a coal bucket because the cold from the floor seeped through her boots. She tried to relax, although that was difficult, with Quinn sitting beside her, his shoulder touching hers. She unzipped her coat. Was it the heat from the stove, or Quinn's presence that caused the sudden flash of warmth?

Quinn hadn't been able to decipher Livia's feelings toward him. Was she angry because he'd ignored her advances when they'd been together before? Since he blamed himself for ending their relationship, it was up to him to apologize. Sensing that he'd hurt Olivia, he proceeded with caution.

Praying for the right words, he said, "I've often wondered what happened to you, Olivia."

She was tempted to answer that he knew where she lived, if he'd wanted to know so badly, but pride kept her from making the comment. Instead, she said, "You might as well call me Livia. Only my parents still use my full name."

"You've always been Olivia in my thoughts, but I'll try to change."

So, he hadn't forgotten everything!

Another long silence.

It seemed obvious that Livia wasn't going to speak, so what should he do now? Often, Quinn had wondered if he'd ever see her again, and a few times he'd considered looking her up, because he knew where she lived. But he'd always pushed aside the idea because he felt guilty about the past. Several years older than her, he should have been aware that Livia was developing a crush on him. But he'd never considered himself an irresistible man, and the thought of her being infatuated with him hadn't entered his mind.

"I've often wanted the chance to apologize for mishandling the situation between us. But you were quite a bit younger than I was, and I didn't—"

"Didn't think I was silly enough to fall in love with a man who hadn't given me any encouragement?" she interrupted bitterly.

"Oh, I'm sure it was only a crush," Quinn protested. "It couldn't have been love. You were just a kid."

"I was seventeen and old enough to know better. But, please, Quinn, that's a period of my life I'd prefer to forget. Consider yourself forgiven, if you think it's necessary, but I'd prefer not to talk about it."

"Then what can we talk about? If we just sit here and stare at the walls, time will pass mighty slowly."

"Let's talk about what we're doing now. I'm studying to be a veterinarian, too. I wanted to do something using my rural upbringing. My brother, Evan, is a county extension agent, and he also does some teaching at a nearby university. My sister is a high school teacher. I wasn't interested in teaching. But I love animals and I've worked with them all of my life. Being a veterinarian was my best choice."

"It isn't easy though, as I'm sure you're finding out."

"I know! I might as well have aspired to become a medical doctor, with all the science and other hard subjects I'm studying."

"After being in school for several years, I decided to stay on the farm for a while. Working as a farrier helps me keep up with my profession. I intend to set up my veterinarian practice in a few months."

Someone coughed, and Livia thought it was Sean. She hoped that this exposure to the severe weather didn't give him a cold. Inside the firebox, a large block of coal crumbled and the pungent smell of smoke permeated the room.

Since the wind seemed less blustery than it had earlier, she asked, "Is there any possibility we'll be rescued tomorrow?"

"I doubt it," Quinn said, with a quick glance toward her. Although Livia's features were shadowed in the dim light, the sadness mirrored on her face made her blue eyes appear almost black. "When we have bad snowstorms like this, the remote areas are always the last to get help. I hope I'm wrong, for your sake and for the others, but it could be several days before we see a snowplow."

"Doesn't it bother you to miss Christmas with your family?"

"Somewhat. But this isn't the first time I've been away from home on Christmas. I've gone skiing in Colorado with my friends several times over the Christmas holidays. My family doesn't go overboard in observing the holiday like a lot of families do. What special things does your family do at Christmas?"

As they talked, Livia realized that they were easily drifting into the close relationship they'd experienced before—a camaraderie that had turned into love on her part. Although the years had dimmed her emotions, she had no doubt that her feelings for Quinn hadn't been just a crush. He was her first, and only, love. Remembering that he'd said "not yet," when someone asked about his marital status probably indicated he was engaged or involved in a serious relationship. She had to guard her heart carefully to avoid reviving the love she'd once had for him.

Realizing that her mind had been wandering, Livia said quickly, "Our family has always had some unique ways to celebrate Christmas. I won't bore you with all the details."

"I won't be bored, I'm sure," he said.

"Mom prepares special, traditional family foods. Christmas Eve is a time for our immediate family, but on Christmas night, our aunts, uncles and cousins come to Heritage Farm, the ancestral home of the family. We sometimes have a hundred or more people. And we always go to church on Christmas Eve for a candlelight service. I'll probably miss that more than anything else."

Quinn stood, flexed his muscles, opened the stove door and replenished the fuel. The firelight glinted from his dark, curly hair as he moved his head. He held his hands out to the warmth of the stove.

"By daylight, we'll probably have a better idea of when we'll be rescued. If it's fairly obvious that it will be a few days, we should plan our own observance of Christmas. We have all we need to do that. Eric is a preacher, so he can prepare a sermon. Your friend, Roxanne, can play the piano, if it's still in good condition. Your group can sing. The rest of us will be the congregation."

Her eyes brightening, Livia said, "That's a wonderful idea! Preparing to celebrate will keep us busy, and we won't have time to feel sorry for ourselves because we're stranded."

When Roxanne and Sean started their shift, Livia went back to her hard, narrow bed with a lighter heart. Her mind was busy with the possibilities of observing Christmas and sleep still eluded her. Also, her thoughts focused on Quinn, and the wonder of seeing him again. She hadn't been mistaken in remembering him as a wonderful companion.

Livia particularly recalled the time when she and Quinn had taken a group of teenagers on a one-day canoeing expedition. A thunderstorm had come up, the creek had flooded, and they couldn't return to the camp. The twelve of them had spent a soggy, miserable night in the open, without tents or sleeping bags. The circumstances were similar to their present experience. And that time, like this one, Quinn was a bright presence for her.

On the other side of the church, Quinn also was awake. He'd recalled Livia as an energetic, fun-loving girl, but she was a woman now—an intriguing, exciting woman. How much had he missed by rebuffing her advances in the past? She'd been too young to make decisions about her future then. Still, if he'd handled the situation differently, if he'd talked to her about her crush and suggested that they remain friends, he could have kept in touch with her. That friendship might have developed into love by this time.

But since he'd discouraged her once, he had the feeling that Livia wouldn't accept if he tried to deepen their relationship now. It wasn't a matter of taking up where they'd left off, for that was apparently painful for Livia, but he definitely didn't want her to go out of his life again. Would these few days of isolation also convince Livia to start over again?

Chapter Four

Livia may have spent a more miserable night in her life, but when she turned on the narrow bench and rolled out on the floor, the night she'd just endured received high marks for misery. The sound of her fall sounded as loud as an earthquake in the church that had been silent all night, except for the noisy, penetrating wind scattering snow around their shelter.

Besides being embarrassed, Livia felt a pain in her knee. Her hope that she hadn't disturbed any of the others was dashed when Sean, who'd spent most of the night on the bench behind her, peered over the seat. His light brown hair looked as if he'd been running his fingers through it for hours. He was wide-awake.

Holding on to the seat and pulling up from the floor, Livia wrapped a blanket around herself and sat on the pew facing Sean.

"Did I wake you?"

"Are you kidding? I've spent a miserable night. I slept a little before Roxanne and I started our shift," Sean said wearily. "Les relieved us early, an hour ago, but I haven't gone to sleep. Did you hurt yourself when you fell?"

"My knee stings a little, but it's no big deal."

Glancing around the room, she saw that some of the others were seated in the pews or hovering around the stove. Marie, a few seats back, caught Livia's eye, and motioned outside. Livia shivered at the thought of making a trip to the necessary, but she would welcome some fresh air. All night long, sporadic bursts of wind had swept down the chimney, blowing smoke into the room, making breathing difficult.

Livia cast the blanket aside, pulled on the heavy coat she'd taken off during the night and picked up her wool gloves. Marie and Roxanne waited by the back door.

"One thing about sleeping in all your clothes, you don't have to make a lot of preparation when you go outdoors," Marie joked.

It took a lot to upset Marie, and Livia wished she could be more like her. She couldn't stop worrying about their situation, and her lack of faith in God's providence annoyed her.

They met Quinn entering the supply room with two buckets of fuel. His shoulders were covered with snow.

"So it's still snowing," Livia said.

"Off and on," Quinn replied. "The worst problem now is the drifting snow. I shoveled the paths clear again, but the wind will no doubt fill them soon. Be careful," he said as he stood aside to let them go out the door.

"Wow!" Livia said as a blast of frigid air almost took her breath away. When they left the shelter of the building, a wind surge staggered her.

"I wanted some fresh air, but this is a little too fresh." She snuggled deeper into her coat and pulled the collar over her mouth.

Marie stopped in front of her, her face showing her awe as she looked around their white world. The branches on several evergreens drooped under the weight of snow. Large mounds of snow covered shrubbery. A foot or more of snow lay on the roofs of the buildings. Livia had seen many heavy snowfalls and their aftermath in rural areas, but to Marie, who had lived in a big city all of her life, this was obviously a wondrous sight.

"The thing that impresses me the most," Marie said, "is the quietness. You know how it is in a city—we never have complete silence. But when the wind ceases for a short time, it's uncanny how quiet it is."

A brilliant cardinal whizzed past them and settled on a snow-laden branch, causing snowflakes to flutter to the ground. The red feathers of the bird stood out vividly against the white landscape.

"Oh, look," Roxanne said, pointing to the cardinal. "Our state bird in all its glory."

The ground beneath the low-spreading spruce tree was clear of snow, and a flock of chattering birds perched in the lower branches.

"If Allen has any bird feed in his truck," Livia said, "I'd like to buy some, and we can put some food out for the birds. This is a difficult time for them to find food."

The frigid wind and the swirling snow hastened their outdoor stay. The church was empty when they returned, except for Eric, who was kneeling in prayer on the platform. The women huddled around the stove, holding out their hands for some heat.

Livia took her cell phone out of her pocket, but still no service was available. "I'll step outside and see if that will help," she said to the others.

She walked a few feet away from the church but couldn't use the phone. She waved to Sean and Quinn who were shoveling nearby. She hurried back to the semiwarm church and shook her head to Marie's questioning look.

"Livia, had you known Quinn before last night?" Marie asked, speaking quietly so as not to disturb her husband. "I sensed some sort of a spark between the two of you."

"It must have been a bright spark to last for three years," Livia tried to joke. "We met several years ago when both of us were on the staff of a 4-H camp. I hadn't seen or heard from him again until last night. It was a surprise to see him."

"Even if we have been singing together for over a year," Roxanne said, "we know so little about each other. I didn't know until last night that you were a farm girl."

Laughing lightly, Marie said, "I have a feeling that we'll know a lot about each other before we're rescued."

"Maybe even things we'd rather not know," her mother agreed.

"Let's try to prepare some breakfast," Livia said. "My stomach is in the habit of having food three times a day."

His devotions finished, Eric joined them near the stove. He kissed Marie and said to Livia, "It's a habit you may have to break if we're here very long."

"Where are the rest of the men?" his wife asked.

"Allen and Les went to the truck to see if they could find some instant coffee. Les insists he can't function until he has his morning cup."

"So that's the reason for the pan of water on the stove," Livia said.

"Yes," Eric said. "Where he unearthed that old pot, I don't know, but he scrubbed it with snow until it was clean enough. He poured a couple of bottles of water in it."

"Good," Roxanne said. "I could use some coffee, too."

"It would be nice to have some hot water for washing," Marie said hopefully. "I don't want to wash my hands in snow."

Eric pointed to a carton of antibacterial hand wipes that Allen had brought in last night. "We'll have to make do with those. We can't risk using our bottled water for washing."

"What's Sean doing?" Roxanne asked.

"Quinn is teaching him how to shovel snow," Eric said with a lopsided grin. "They're cleaning off the steps and the porch. He's doing quite well for a guy from Southern California."

As if on cue, the door opened and Sean entered.

"I don't know how you people have survived over the years in this kind of weather," he said as he stomped his feet to remove the snow. "No wonder my family left the Midwest and moved to California. But why did my dad, who's an alumni of OSU, insist that I follow in his footsteps?"

Although Sean spoke in a light tone, Livia sympathized with him. He was suffering with the low temperatures more than the rest of them.

"Where's Quinn?" she asked.

"He went to his truck, while Allen and Les are down there. He and Les are very insistent that none of us should leave this building alone."

"Can you see the vehicles from here?" Marie asked.

"No. The visibility is less than ten feet. It isn't snowing right now, but the wind is whipping the feathery flakes until it looks like we're having another blizzard."

A smile graced Les's wrinkled face when he walked in a few minutes later. He held up a jar of ground coffee. "We had to hunt for a long time before we found it," he said. "Is the water hot?"

Roxanne laid an experimental finger on the side of the pan. "Warm, but not hot."

"I'll put another log or two on the fire," Les said.

"I'm trying to be sparin' of the fuel. We might be here several days, and we don't want to run out, but I've got to have my coffee."

"A sausage biscuit would taste pretty good right now," Sean said. "Have you got one of those tucked away in your coat pocket?"

Although Les was friendly to everyone else, he seemed to dislike Sean, and he snapped, "No, city boy, you're gonna have to rough it like the rest of us."

Sean exchanged a quick glance with Roxanne and shrugged his shoulders. Livia knew Sean had been joking. In fact, under the circumstances, she thought the basketball player was adjusting quite well to the situation. She touched Sean's hand.

"He's one of those people who's grouchy before he has a cup of coffee," she whispered. "He'll probably be all right after we've eaten."

Sean responded by giving Livia a quick hug just as Quinn stepped into the door. Livia felt her face flushing as Quinn observed the gesture with obscure curiosity. Quinn's day-old stubble was frosted with snowflakes, and he looked unbelievably handsome to Livia.

She moved quickly away from Sean and joined Roxanne and Marie, who were examining the boxes of food the men had brought from the truck.

"Here are some individual boxes of cereal," Roxanne said. "We put the milk in the supply room, and it will be cold enough for us to use on our cereal." She set out a box of doughnuts.

"We have some juice in individual containers, too," Marie said. "We're fortunate to have this much."

"I started my truck and picked up a weather report on the radio," Quinn said. "I wish I had better news, but there's another round of snow coming this afternoon and twenty-below temperatures predicted for tonight."

The very thought caused cold chills to run up and down Livia's spine. The little church had been frigid *last* night, and that meant it would get worse.

"What about our chances of being rescued?" Eric asked, with a quick glance at his wife.

Quinn shook his head. "Several counties in this area are completely isolated. No rescue today, I'm sure."

"So not only will we be away from home on Christmas Eve and Christmas Day, we may not get out of here for several days," Allen said.

"Looks like," Quinn said.

"I wish there was some way to let my wife know I'm all right," Allen said. "But I suppose all of you have the same concern."

Quinn moved to Livia's side. "I'm sorry you can't get home," he said quietly.

"Yeah, me, too," she agreed. "But things could be a lot worse."

If she couldn't be at Heritage Farm for Christmas, she welcomed this time with Quinn.

"Have you said anything about our plans to celebrate Christmas?"

She shook her head. "Let's wait until they've had

some breakfast. They might be more responsive to the idea then."

By the time they'd eaten their cereal and doughnuts, the water was hot enough for coffee. The coffee drinkers sipped on their favorite beverage from disposable cups, a sense of satisfaction on their faces. Marie and Livia didn't like coffee, so they drank juice.

They finished eating by nine o'clock, with a long day looming before them. The room was dim because the overcast skies kept the sun hidden. The candles had been extinguished to preserve them, as well as to improve the oxygen in the room.

In spite of heavy socks and boots, Livia's feet felt numb. She put her hand on the cold wooden floor, and knew that the heat from the stove would never warm it. The church was built only a few feet off the ground, and it was doubtful if there was any insulation underneath the building.

She went to her pack and found a comb. Even in the building, she'd kept the hood over her head most of the time. Her hair was knotted and twisted. She combed the tangles out as best she could, but wasn't making much progress when Sean sat down behind her and took the comb from her hand.

"Here, let me help," he said, "I have two younger sisters, and my mother always made me comb their hair. I got so good at it that I once considered becoming a barber." Perhaps comparing that occupation with the opportunity to become a professional basketball player, he laughed jovially. "Give me the comb and I'll be *your* big brother today." He worked gently with her hair until it flowed softly over her shoulders. When she turned toward the group near the stove, Quinn was looking at her. He turned his eyes away quickly. *What must he be thinking?*

Watching the shivering people circling the stove, Livia doubted that there'd be much interest in having a Christmas celebration. The others probably felt as miserable as she did, and she knew it would be tempting just to sit, stew and feel sorry for themselves.

Quinn raised questioning eyebrows to her, and she nodded. "You go ahead," she mouthed to him.

"Hey, folks," Quinn said. "Livia and I came up with an idea last night. Since it's pretty obvious that we can't get home for Christmas, we thought we should overcome our difficulties and celebrate Christmas here."

The other snowbound travelers looked around at each other. Seeing the dejection in their eyes, even if it wasn't necessarily showing in their facial expressions, Livia said, "Come on, everyone. Christmas is more than time spent with family. Let's make a stab at happiness. How many are willing to remember the true reason we celebrate Christmas?"

Chapter Five

Silence greeted Livia's question until Roxanne said, "Your suggestion makes sense, but I'm not sure I can get in the spirit of Christmas."

"Me, either," Sean said, and Les gave a derisive snort. Sean continued as if he hadn't heard Les. "Two days ago if anyone had told me that my most desired gift would be something as simple as a shower and a shave, I'd have thought they were crazy."

"Twon't hurt you none to go without a bath for a day or two," Les said, frowning at Sean, before he turned away. "I think you've got a good idea, Quinn." He looked around the church fondly. "It's been a long time since Christmas carols have been sung inside these walls. I kinda think the old church would welcome a Christmas Eve service."

With a shrewd glance from Sean to Les, Allen said, "Except for gifts and such, I don't know much about celebrating Christmas. However, I've learned a lot about human nature in my thirty-five years. If we sit around worrying about being cold, needing a bath, and being afraid we'll run out of food and fuel, we're going to get on each other's nerves. We'd better do *something*."

Since Eric was the only minister among them, all eyes turned to him. He stood and walked around the room. The others watched him, waiting for his decision. He lifted the lid of the upright piano and ran his fingers over the keys. Roxanne shuddered. Livia was amused that the out-of-tune piano grated on the pianist's nerves.

Eric stared at the stained-glass window. He stood behind the lectern, his hands on the dusty top.

"Until we're faced with a situation like this," he began, "we often forget the real meaning of Christmas and why we observe it." With a lopsided grin, he continued, "Standing in this pulpit brings out the preacher in me. I'm sure all of you know that the Bible doesn't say anything about celebrating the birth of Jesus. It's not His *birth,* but His death, burial and resurrection that holds the key to our salvation. We need to keep that truth foremost in our minds."

A strong blast of wind rattled the window frames. Sitting beside Sean, Livia felt him shiver.

"It was the fourth century before Christians started observing His birth, which coincided with a Roman pagan holiday, the Saturnalia, celebrated near the winter solstice. The exact date of the birth of Christ is uncertain, but by the Middle Ages, the twenty-fifth of December was generally accepted as Christmas Day."

"As I remember from Sunday school," Livia said, "early observances consisted mostly of feasting and merrymaking, a lot like the way people celebrate today."

Eric nodded. "At first, a few churches honored the nativity for one day. But during the Middle Ages, celebrations expanded to a week or two. During the Protestant Reformation, in the sixteenth century, Christmas *had* become a day of reveling more than a time of worship. The celebration was outlawed by many religious sects."

"That includes the Pilgrims and Puritans," Quinn added. "They didn't observe Christmas, but other Europeans brought the worship of Christmas to our shores. Since the Bible doesn't specifically tell us when and where, or even *if* we should observe the birth of Jesus, we can worship here as well as if we were in our own church buildings."

"As I said earlier," Eric continued, "I personally feel that God brought us together in this place for some specific reason. We can each observe the holiday in our own way, or we can join together in a unique experience that will bring us closer to the real meaning of Christmas and to each other. Are you with me?"

Everyone applauded, and Sean said, "How do we start?"

"I want to have a tree," Allen said. "I've always decorated the tree with my kids. As soon as it's light enough, I'll check outside and see if I can find anything that will serve as a tree."

"No reason you can't cut some branches off the evergreens in the cemetery," Les said. "We have to trim the trees every few years anyway."

"I've got a sewing kit in the van," Roxanne said. "If you've got any bags of popcorn in the truck, we can string that into a garland."

"I know there are some cranberries you can string with the corn," Allen said.

"Let's draw names like we did in elementary school," Livia said. "Surely, we can sort through our belongings and come up with eight gifts, even if some of the things are used. Maybe we can use whatever talents we have to give gifts that will help us remember this experience with fondness."

"I'm for that," Allen said. "I'm trying to deal with this situation positively. But I feel like an outsider. Five of you are friends. Les and I are kinda separated from the rest of you. I'm trying not to think of the negative things, like the damage to the truck and missing my family. But it's hard."

Eric stepped to Allen's side and put a brotherly arm around his broad shoulders. "My friend, we're all in this together. Don't feel shut out. Fortunately, I have my wife and mother-in-law with me. But I'm concerned about my parents, who'll be very worried about us. *We* know we're all right, but they don't. In many ways, they're going to have a worse holiday than we will. I've been praying that God will give our families peace of mind."

It seemed odd to see tears appear in Allen's eyes. His

appearance suggested that he was the rugged he-man type, who wouldn't be daunted by any situation.

"Buddy," Les said, "I'm alone, too, but somehow when I'm in this old church, I feel a kinship with my loved ones who worshiped here, but who've gone on to a better place."

Perhaps considering that the conversation could turn negative, Eric said, "Shall we plan our worship service to end at midnight?"

"Good idea. We want to stay up as long as we can," Les agreed. "If we're movin' around, we won't feel the cold as much."

"While we've been talking," Quinn said, "I heard a helicopter flying over. It's probably the National Guard looked for stranded vehicles. We may have been spotted already. When we go out, we can clean the snow off the side of the church van, so the name can be seen by searchers. I've also been praying that God will reassure our families."

"I'm for making gifts for one another," Sean said. "I've got something in mind, but I doubt I can get it finished today. Let's wait until tomorrow morning to open our presents."

"I have some gifts in the truck I was taking home with me," Quinn said. "Under the circumstances, my family won't mind if I share them with you. If anyone can't think of a gift, you're welcome to anything I have."

"Don't forget to look for things in the supply room," Les said. "There might be something left from years gone by to make gifts or Christmas decorations. We used to have big Christmas programs here."

"Eric, while you plan a message," Roxanne said, "I'll see if I can get any music out of the piano. If not, we'll sing a capella."

"You might try the organ," Les suggested.

"I've already checked out the organ," Roxanne said with a laugh. "It's a pump organ. I've never tried to play one of them."

"No time like the present," Les said, as he picked up the fuel buckets and headed for the back door.

Roxanne sat on the circular organ stool, lifted the covering over the keys, and pulled out several of the regulating stops above the keyboard. Livia heard her giggling as she pumped up and down on the squeaking pedals, but her fingers picked out a melody that Livia recognized as "Silent Night."

"My boots keep sliding on these pedals. And if I forget to pump, I don't get any music," Roxanne said. "No wonder the pioneers were so hardy. This organ would make an excellent leg exerciser. But I think I'd better use the piano for tonight's service, even if it's not in tune."

"Mom," Marie said, "you know you can get music out of a washboard. It'll sound great."

And although the piano did sound out of tune to an experienced ear, in a short time, the strains of traditional Christmas music sounded through the room. Sean stood beside the piano, and he and Roxanne started singing the lyrics. The music lent a sense of gaiety to the stranded travelers, who went about their tasks humming or singing with them.

"Jingle bells, jingle bells, jingle all the way. Oh what fun it is to ride in a one-horse open sleigh," Livia sang as she rummaged in her purse for paper and pen.

Quinn came to the front pew and sat beside her. "Too bad we don't have a sleigh and the horse. We could get out of our predicament a little easier."

"We have a sleigh and plenty of horses on Heritage Farm," Livia said, finding it didn't hurt as much to talk about home when Quinn was beside her. "In fact, three years ago when my brother, Evan, brought his girlfriend, Wendy, home for a visit, they went to the Christmas Eve service in a sleigh that belonged to my grandfather. Evan and Wendy got married the following spring, and they have a little boy now."

"Someone to carry on the Kessler name then. I remember you told me about the family traditions when we met."

Livia's face flushed, and she recalled again the acute humiliation she'd lived with for years. It was time for her to stop dwelling on the negative. She must think about the good things of their past relationship rather than that last, embarrassing day.

"We've already learned that Derek has a mind of his own," she said. "He's a very strong-willed child, and he may start new family traditions, rather than carry on the old."

"Hey, Quinn," Les said when he came back with the

fuel, "that extra blizzard last night brought six more inches of snow. Time to start shoveling."

Quinn groaned under his breath. "Les is a hard task-master. If he'd wait until the wind stops, we wouldn't have so much shoveling to do. And he shouldn't be shoveling snow at his age, but…to keep peace in our gathered family, I'll do what he says." He touched her shoulder, saying, "Keep your chin up."

The touch of his hand sent a ripple of excitement through her body.

Livia cut eight strips of paper from her notebook and wrote the names of each of the travelers on one. What if she should get Quinn's name? For the past three years, she'd often seen gifts that she would have liked to buy for him, when shopping for friends and family.

She folded the slips of paper and dropped them into an offering tray that she found inside the lectern. She mixed the names and passed them around, then took the last paper. It was Sean's name, and she didn't know whether she was pleased or not. She would have liked an excuse to give Quinn a gift, but Sean would be more appreciative of the wool scarf she'd been knitting for her brother.

By noon, the sun was shining. The reflection on the snow was blinding, and no one dared go outside without sunglasses. Livia put hers on and stepped out on the little porch, enjoying a good look at their surroundings.

Quinn and Allen had finally persuaded Les to leave the shoveling to them, and they'd cleared an area around the front steps, as well as the area in the back where the woodshed and necessaries were located.

The landscape was awesome. Livia could see their vehicles about forty yards from the church. Across the road, a few headstones extending out of the snow marked the location of the cemetery. A large number of cedar and pine trees intermingled with the grave markers. The land was relatively flat with a few knolls toward the east.

The sun did nothing to warm the bone-chilling atmosphere. When Livia breathed deeply, the cold air nearly suffocated her. She zipped her coat high enough to cover the lower half of her face.

"We can get frostbite if we stay out too long," Quinn said quietly at her elbow. "I don't want to frighten our companions, but I'm more concerned now than I was before. We have only enough fuel to last two more days."

"That's why it's important to keep them focused on observing Christmas to get their minds off things. I keep thinking it could be so much worse."

"What's Allen doing in the cemetery?" Roxanne asked from her stance on the steps.

Livia hadn't noticed him because he was covered with snow and faded into the white landscape. Allen was cutting branches off of a cedar tree with a handsaw. Every movement of his hand dislodged a small avalanche of snow that landed on his shoulders.

"He's getting greenery for a Christmas tree," Quinn explained. "He found the saw in the woodshed. I'm

going to the truck now. I have a gift that will be suit-
able for the person whose name I've drawn. I won't
have to make anything."

"Don't stay out too long," Livia cautioned.

"I won't. My feet and hands are already cold."

He held open the door for Livia to enter the building. Their shoulders touched, their eyes met, and the
sudden warmth in his gaze caused Livia to look away
in confusion.

Chapter Six

Quinn closed the door and paused with his hand still holding the doorknob. An unfamiliar shiver of awareness seized his body. He knew a tense magnetism was kindling between him and Livia.

Stamping his feet to keep the circulation going, Quinn picked up a big stick that leaned against the church to use as a cane as he broke ground to his truck. When he'd been shopping two days ago for his family's gifts, he'd seen a music box with a twirling angel on top. As he'd listened to the song, "Angels We Have Heard on High," Quinn felt compelled to buy the gift, although he had no idea who he'd give it to. Now that he'd drawn Livia's name, it seemed the perfect gift for her. He'd had the music box gift-wrapped in the store, so all he had to do was put her name on it.

Quinn returned to the church in time to help Allen shape the three branches of cedar into the semblance of a tree. They used chunks of coal and wood to secure the branches in a discarded bucket they'd found in the woodshed. They wrapped the bucket in a red silk scarf that Livia provided.

Humming a Christmas tune, Marie strung the cranberries and popcorn into a garland. Les had found a box of old ornaments and some tinsel in the supply room, which Livia draped over their tree. She arranged one candle on each windowsill among some pieces of shrubbery not needed for the tree.

Laughing at their feeble efforts at making decorations, Marie said, "This just proves the old saying, 'poor people have poor ways, and lots of 'em.'"

Livia stood back to survey their handiwork. "Oh, I don't know," she said. "Our decorations are festive."

"To say the least," Marie said, with another laugh, and joined Sean and Roxanne, who were still practicing at the piano.

While the others had decorated, Eric wrapped up in a blanket and sat on a pew beneath the stained-glass window. He studied his Bible and took notes on his message for the evening service.

Food, such as it was, was set out on one of the pews, and throughout the day, people ate when they wanted to. No one seemed to have much of an appetite, but they were keeping busy, either making gifts or wrapping what they'd found in their belongings.

Eric and Quinn made another trip to the vehicles before dark to get a shopping bag of things Roxanne had bought in Detroit. She took out a package of wrapping paper and some tape. "You can all use this. I'll put it on a table in the supply room, and you can sneak in there to do your wrapping if you want to keep your presents secret."

Little by little, wrapped gifts appeared under the makeshift tree.

When the sun shone through the dirty windows of the church, Livia felt almost happy as she hurried to finish the scarf she was making for Sean. But as darkness approached, she accepted the fact that she would not be home for Christmas Day.

Her mother, Hilda, had always been the strong one of the family, the lodestar that kept her children close to home. But Hilda had also given her children freedom to be independent and make their own decisions. Livia could almost believe that she heard her mother's voice telling her to make the best of the situation.

Considering the ages of her companions, Livia realized that she was the youngest of the group, just as she always was at home. She'd rather liked being the baby of the Kessler family, but when Quinn had hinted that he hadn't pursued a relationship with her because he was older than she was, Livia would have welcomed adding a few years to her age.

When Allen brought in the bag of sunflower seeds that Livia asked him to bring, Quinn found an old can in the woodshed and filled it with the seeds. He took a shovel and went with Livia to the backyard. He scooped the snow from the ground under the evergreens, and Livia scattered the seed in several piles. Companionably, they stood shoulder to shoulder and watched the chickadees, cardinals, woodpeckers and sparrows hungrily dive into the black seeds.

"This is something else we share," Quinn said. "We have several bird feeders on our farm, and apparently you do also."

The more she was around Quinn, Livia realized that they did have a lot in common—their rural background being one of the most important.

"Yes, we feed the birds year-round, and we always have flocks of them."

When they returned to the building, Eric was questioning Les about the architecture of the church.

"There's a steeple on the church, so it must have had a bell at one time," Eric commented.

Les motioned toward a small square door in the ceiling. "It's still up there, but there ain't been a rope on it for a long time. It was a pretty-soundin' bell."

"Too bad we can't ring it," Eric said. "It would be a nice addition to our worship service tonight. Also, if we ring the bell, people living in the area might hear it and come to help us."

"That's a possibility, Eric," Quinn said. "I've got a twenty-foot rope in my pickup. And didn't I see a ladder in the woodshed, Les?"

"Yeah. It's kinda old and rickety, but I think we can use it."

With Les standing on the steps watching him, Quinn made another trip to his truck for the rope. Allen volunteered to climb the ladder and attach the rope. When he opened the trapdoor and stepped out on the timbers of the balcony, he shouted down to the others, "Let's hurry this up. It feels like the North Pole up here. We don't want to let a lot of cold air into the building."

Quinn tossed the rope up to him. Following Les's instructions on where to attach the rope to the bell, Allen soon dropped the rope through the small hole cut in the ceiling for that purpose. He closed the door and clambered down the ladder.

Handing the end of the rope to Les, Quinn said, "You do the honors, Les."

Holding the rope in his hand, Les hesitated. "I've been having second thoughts about ringing the bell. I should have told you to check the wooden structure, Allen. That bell weighs about a thousand pounds, and the timbers that hold it are old. I'm not sure how strong they are. If they give way and the bell falls through the ceiling, we'll not have a roof over our head. As the old sayin' goes, 'We'd be up the creek without a paddle.' We're gonna need all the protection we can get tonight."

"Don't ring it then, if that's the case," Eric said.

"I hate to throw cold water on the idea," Les said.

"I can go up and check out the timbers," Quinn said. "I should be able to tell if they're stable."

"That would be wise," Les agreed. "My old legs are too unsteady to climb the ladder, or I'd go. You're a muscular guy, Quinn, so watch where you step."

Fearful for Quinn, Livia said, "If it's so dangerous, maybe we shouldn't ring the bell."

He glanced her way. "It'll be all right," he assured her. "I've climbed around in barn lofts since I was a kid. This won't be much different."

Quinn's stomach was flat and his hips slender, but his shoulders were brawny. While his muscular physique stood him in good stead professionally when handling horses, cows and other large animals, Livia wondered if his shoulders were too wide to crawl through the trapdoor.

He set his right foot on the first rung. The old wooden ladder creaked under his weight, as it had under Allen's. Livia held her breath until Quinn climbed the ten feet and squeezed through the small opening. She heard his steps as he moved from rafter to rafter circling the bell tower.

Les stood under the opening, his eyes squinted tightly, trying to see what was going on.

"How does the wooden frame look?" he called.

On his hands and knees now, Quinn peered through the opening. "Solid as a rock," he assured Les. "But while I'm up here, I'll take a look at the flue and be sure it's all right. We don't want to risk a fire."

Quinn crawled carefully toward the flue, wishing he'd brought a flashlight. He ran his hands over the bricks, and while he felt some warmth, it wasn't more than would be expected after the stove had been burning for hours. Turning toward the ladder, he hit his head on a beam, his foot slipped off the rafter and he fell hard. Pain ran up his left leg as it plunged through the ceiling.

Lath and plaster fell on the group waiting below, and Livia stifled a cry as Quinn's leg, up to his knee, hung through the ceiling. Quickly, Allen climbed the ladder.

"Are you hurt, Quinn?" he called, sticking his head into the attic.

"Not much," Quinn gasped, "but I sure got a scare. I was afraid I'd come through the ceiling."

"Do you need any help?"

"I'll see if I can make it by myself," Quinn said. He wiggled backward, keenly aware of a sharp nail that tore the seat of his pants. He carefully pulled his leg out of the hole. He wiggled his foot, thankful that he didn't seem to have broken a bone. No doubt the heavy boots and socks he wore had prevented any serious damage.

"Allen, I'll crawl toward you, but before I come down, we'd better put something over that hole in the ceiling to keep the cold air out of the room. See if there's a board to cover it, or perhaps we can use one of our blankets."

Allen came down a few rungs on the ladder. "Eric, bring one of our blankets, so he can fill the hole."

Eric grabbed the first blanket he found and gave it to Allen, who in turn handed it to Quinn. Aware of the pain in his leg, and hoping he didn't have a serious injury, he crawled back to the hole and covered it.

Both Eric and Allen held the ladder as Quinn started down. When he put his weight on his left leg, a pain shot from his ankle to his hip, and he almost fell from the ladder. Gritting his teeth and holding tightly to each rung, he reached the floor without any further incident.

He held Allen's arm as he walked to the nearest pew and sat down.

Alarmed by the pallor on his face, Livia hurried to him. "You've hurt your leg, haven't you?"

"'Fraid so," he admitted. "I shouldn't have been so clumsy."

She knelt beside him and started unlacing his boot. Sean joined her, and helped her pull off Quinn's boot and sock. His fingers moved quickly and gingerly over Quinn's cold foot and leg.

"Sean has had training with injuries like this," Livia explained. "It comes in handy in basketball training and during the games, too."

"I don't believe you have any broken bones," Sean said. "I think it's a sprain or an injured muscle. Try to stand and walk a little."

With his hand on Sean's shoulder, Quinn took several steps. "Is the pain bad?" Livia asked.

Quinn shook his head. "It's uncomfortable, but I'm sure I'll be all right. Sorry to cause such a commotion," he apologized to the others.

"I'll bet you stepped on the place where the stovepipe used to go through the ceiling," Les said. "The stovepipe went straight up then, but we decided to put a curved ell extension when we bought this new stove. We just patched the ceiling when we finished, and I forgot that place would be weak."

When Livia walked away, Quinn checked out the rip in his pants. Pointing to a pew on the other side of the aisle, Quinn quietly said to Allen, "There's a pair of jeans in my pack under that seat. Will you bring them? I tore my pants. I'll go to the supply room and change them."

Although Quinn tried to be nonchalant, the episode had embarrassed him. He didn't like to be the center of attention. But was it worth having ripped pants and a sore leg to witness Livia's obvious concern for him? Could he dare to hope that her anxiety indicated a kind feeling in her heart for him?

Chapter Seven

When her pulse stopped pounding from the trauma of Quinn's fall, Livia sat on the front pew and picked up her needlework. Quinn watched her, studying each feature of her face. Should he capitalize on her anxiety over his fall and try to lessen the tension between them?

More than a century of grime had accumulated in the attic, and as Quinn surveyed his hands, it looked as if most of it had rubbed off on him. He cleaned his hands with several hand wipes before he changed his pants. When he came from the supply room, he looked around for Livia.

He limped toward her. "May I join you?" he said. "Everyone is determined to treat me like an invalid and won't let me work. Eric and Allen are bringing in the fuel, and Sean is shoveling the drifted snow. I think we could make a country boy out of him if we tried."

Quinn was concerned about some of the gestures

he'd noticed between Sean and Livia. Sean was close to her age, and so likeable that Quinn wouldn't blame any girl for choosing him.

She moved the basket of yarn from the seat, and critically examined the stitches she'd made, She found it difficult to ply the needle in and out of the yarn because her fingers were cold.

"Sit down. This gift isn't for you, so you can watch if you like."

He sat beside her and stretched out his left leg. He watched her long, sensitive fingers as she wielded the metal crochet hook through the red wool yarn.

"I was making this for my brother," Livia said, interrupting his thoughts, "but since I drew Sean's name, I'm finishing it for his gift. Evan won't mind. I've made him several scarves."

"Does Evan manage Heritage Farm?" he asked.

"Daddy and Evan are in partnership. Daddy does most of the managing, but he's semiretired. Evan and his family live on the farm. He also has a full-time job as county extension agent, so he's very busy. His wife, Wendy, has a teaching degree. She taught school for two years, but she decided to become a stay-at-home mom when Derek was born. Wendy's maternal grandparents came to spend Christmas with her, but they couldn't stay long. I hope I don't miss seeing them."

"You invited me once to visit Heritage Farm. I'm sorry I didn't make it."

Livia hesitated, not knowing what to say. She double-crocheted a few inches, made a turn, and started the last row on the scarf.

"You'd be welcome anytime. It's a good farm with fertile river land and some hill acreage. You'd like my family, I'm sure."

"I'll take you up on that invitation before long. I hope we can stay in touch now. If you'll give me your telephone number, I can call you once in a while. And as far as that's concerned, it's not so far to Columbus that I couldn't drive in to see you occasionally."

His comment flustered Livia, and she concentrated on her needlework. She stretched out the scarf and decided it was long enough. To put on the finishing touches, she took a skein of white yarn from her basket to make a border of single crochet stitches around the whole scarf. Fortunately, she didn't need to count this simple stitch. Quinn's comments had disconcerted her, and she was tormented by confusing emotions when she sat so close to him.

Should she ask Quinn about his personal life? If he was romantically involved with someone else, she'd see to it that she wasn't at home when he visited Heritage Farm. She'd never told her family about her infatuation with Quinn, but it was hard to fool her family. Her mother had sensed something had happened at the camp, but had never asked. If they saw Quinn and her together, they would immediately know they were dating.

"When you introduced yourself last night," she said, and her fingers gripped the crochet hook tightly, "you said you weren't married *yet*. Does that mean you're intending to get married soon?"

She sure didn't want Quinn to bring his wife to Heritage Farm.

Quinn squirmed on the hard seat, conscious of the nail scratch he'd gotten in the attic.

"No, I'm not. I've been dating a neighbor I grew up with, but we're not serious. Mostly, we're just friends."

She didn't answer, seemingly concentrating on her crocheting, but her mind was whirling.

"What about you?" he asked. "I've noticed a closeness between you and Sean."

She stared at him, complete surprise on her face. "Sean! We're friends—nothing more. He has too much on his plate keeping in shape for basketball and maintaining good grades to be interested in girls. Not that a lot of women wouldn't welcome his attention."

"Including you," Quinn persisted.

Livia crocheted several more stitches, her mind spinning with bewilderment. Could he possibly be jealous of Sean? The thought was heartening.

She shook her head, repeating, "Sean and I are friends. I haven't dated since I was in high school."

"Why?"

She shrugged one shoulder and managed to say casually, "I haven't met anyone I wanted to date."

He laughed slightly. "That a good reason, I suppose."

He stood cautiously, and she believed he was hurt more than he'd admit. "I won't bother you anymore so you can finish your work."

She let him go without further comment.

Roxanne had humorously appointed herself as the chef, and she asked Allen to bring a case of canned vegetable soup from his truck.

"Every time I see how much eight people can eat," she said to Livia, "I'm thankful for that truckload of food. Those few snacks we had in the car wouldn't have lasted long."

Les contributed a large pan that he was taking as a gift to his daughter, and they opened ten cans of the soup and dumped it into the pan. It took more than an hour before the soup was edible, and then it was only lukewarm.

The soup, along with cheese, bread, crackers, apples and cookies, sated their hunger temporarily. Livia had never been a big eater, but she knew she would be hungry before morning. They had divided the soup into eight equal shares, and she figured it did little to appease the appetites of Quinn and Allen, both big men, who would obviously require more food than the others.

The little church, with the smell of smoke and food aromas, seemed oppressive for a moment to Livia, and she wanted to be alone. She opened the door and stepped out on the porch. A quarter-moon shed a soft silvery radiance over the little valley where they were marooned.

Although the exact date of Jesus' birth was unknown, it was not inconceivable to believe that He was born on such a night as this. It took only a few minutes for the intense cold to seep through her clothes, and Livia hurried back inside. Quinn slanted a questioning, concerned glance toward her. His gray eyes held hers until she nodded that she was all right.

In preparation for the worship service, Marie and Livia lit the candles in the windows and set another candle on the piano to give Roxanne enough light to find the right keys. The men pulled the piano close to the stove.

"We have our quintet music in the van," Roxanne said, "but it's a difficult arrangement, and I can't see well enough to read the notes. All of us will sing traditional carols, which I can play without music. There are hymnals in the pews, and you can use those if you don't remember the words. Sean will solo 'O Holy Night' at the end of our service."

They all hovered as near the stove as they could when Eric started the service.

"My friends," he said, "I'll ask you first of all to recall a Christmas of the past that's still vivid in your memory."

Livia didn't even have to take a second thought. It was the one they were without electric power several days before Christmas. It was the same year Wendy came to meet the Kessler family. At first, they'd thought it was a disaster to be without electricity. But the days without modern conveniences had drawn them closer together than if circumstances had been normal. Livia thought the same thing was happening in this little forsaken church tonight.

"I can tell by some of your expressions," Eric continued, "that you're having difficulty recalling any specific Christmas that stands out in your memory. Most of my Christmases have been the same. But it goes without saying that this Christmas will never be forgotten. Every year, we'll remember what happened here tonight. We'll talk of it to our children and grandchildren, and they will in turn pass the story on to their families. So it's important that we remember, not only the hardships we endured, and the fellowship we have, but also that we commemorated the birth of Jesus."

Eric prayed, and then he turned to Roxanne.

"Go ahead with your music."

As cold as it was in the room, Livia wondered how Roxanne could play the piano. She wore a pair of thin leather gloves, but they would provide little warmth against the cold black and white keys.

Roxanne's fingers did stumble a little. Livia noticed that she hit several wrong notes, which seldom happened, but the music seemed more beautiful to Livia than when she listened to Roxanne play the Steinway Grand in their church sanctuary. They moved from one well-known carol to another, most of them singing from memory because the candlelight was dim.

More than ever before, Livia envisioned the actual events of the birth of Christ, as Eric read from the second chapter of Luke.

"'And Joseph also went up from Galilee, out of the city of Nazareth, into Judæa, unto the city of David, which is called Bethlehem; to be taxed with Mary his espoused wife, being great with child. And so it was, that, while they were there, the days were accomplished that she should be delivered. And she brought forth her firstborn son, and wrapped Him in swaddling clothes, and laid Him in a manger; because there was no room for them in the inn.'"

Mary would have endured the same pain that any other mother would experience during the birth of her son. Compared to present-day hospital conditions, the Son of God had come into the world under dismal circumstances. But, since He was God in the *flesh,* it was fitting for His birth to be a natural one.

As Eric continued reading the account of Jesus' birth, Livia imagined herself walking with the shepherds as they left the fields and hurried to the stable to see the Christ Child. Tonight, when they were worshiping in a cold, abandoned building, she fully comprehended the pathetic conditions surrounding Joseph and Mary, and their newborn child.

"The focus of my message tonight is based on a verse in the fourth chapter of Galatians," Eric said, interrupting her thoughts. He then read out,"'But when the fullness of the time was come, God sent forth His Son, made of a woman, made under the law.'"

"The Jews had been watching centuries for the promised Messiah," Eric said, "and some had given up hope of His coming. Although men had despaired of His arrival, Jesus came to earth at the *right* time, the *best* time.

"I pray that tonight's message will make a lasting

impression on all of us. Always remember that when God does a work in our lives, it's at the *best* time for us."

A candle in one of the windows tipped over, and Quinn moved quickly to extinguish it before the greenery caught fire. Everyone was conscious of the need to prevent a fire tonight. Eric paused until he returned.

"I don't know where some of you are in your walk with God, but if you feel comfortable in doing so, please kneel with me to worship the newborn King. Each time we worship Jesus, He's born again in our hearts. While we're kneeling, Sean will close our service by singing, 'O Holy Night.'"

When she slid to her knees, Livia realized that Quinn was kneeling beside her. It seemed natural for them to clasp hands.

Before he sang, Sean said, "Although I thought I really wanted to be home in California tonight, I've realized that there's no place I'd rather be than where I am. I've never understood before what the shepherds must have experienced as they knelt before the infant Jesus. I feel sure that the rest of my life, each Christmas Eve, my heart and my thoughts will return to this place."

Livia felt the same way, and the way Quinn squeezed her hand, she knew his thoughts were in harmony with hers.

Singing without musical accompaniment, Sean's strong tenor voice sounded loud and clear in the quiet of the little sanctuary. The only other sound was the popping of coals in the stove.

As he sang the words of the second stanza, Livia's heart sang with him.

"With humble hearts we bow in adoration before this Child, gift of God's matchless love. Sent from on high to purchase our salvation—that we might dwell with him ever above."

When the last strains of the music ceased, a hush fell over the room.

When they stood, Eric said, "Again, don't feel uncomfortable or obligated if it this isn't natural for you, but in our church, we always give hugs of fellowship." He turned to Sean. They embraced and thumped one another on their backs. Livia quivered at Quinn's nearness, wanting him to embrace her, but hardly daring to hope that he would.

"May I?" he asked quietly.

Livia had often fantasized about what it would be like to be held in Quinn's arms. Her body trembled when he pulled her close, and she locked her arms momentarily around his waist.

Quinn sensed that she was trembling, and he wondered if the cold had caused her to shake, or if she also experienced the exhilarating sensations he felt. Uncertain of Livia's feelings, he didn't tighten the embrace as he wanted to do.

Exercising a lot of willpower, Livia removed herself from Quinn's arms and moved to hug the members of her church. Allen and Les were obviously ill at ease with being hugged, though they didn't invite nor rebuff the fellowship gesture.

"Since we're sure that the bell is stable now, how about ringing it to acknowledge the birth of our Savior?" Les said. "I doubt anyone will hear it except us, but we ought to have bells of some kind ringing."

"I keep thinking how God sent angels to the shepherds to tell them the good news of Jesus' birth and where to find Him," Quinn said. "Maybe God will use the ringing bell as a message to people in this area that someone is stranded in the church. By the way, how far is it to nearest house?"

"Oh, no more than five miles," Les answered. "Actually, it's only seven or eight miles west, as the crow flies, to the main highway."

"As clear and still as it is now, the sound of that bell should carry well," Eric said. "Give it a try, Les, and we'll see what it sounds like."

"Stand back, just in case," Les said as he positioned himself under the bell tower and tugged on the rope. The swaying of the bell shook the ceiling, and Livia held her breath, fearing that the bell might fall through the roof.

After a half dozen or so tugs on the rope, the mellow tone of the old bell resounded loud and clear through the church.

"Sounds just like old times," Les said, when he handed the rope to Quinn. "Give it a tug or two, buddy. It's hard pullin' and takes my wind."

As Quinn continue to ring the bell, Roxanne said, "Doesn't it sound beautiful! It's what we needed to bring our worship to a close."

"We should ring it at intervals tomorrow," Quinn said as he let go of the rope. "That bell may bring us some rescuers."

"Since we're running low on fuel," Les said, "I'm thinkin' we'd better bank the fire tonight while we're asleep. We can wrap in blankets and stay warm."

"I've got an idea that might keep us warmer," Quinn said. "Why don't we put the seats of these pews together and two of us sleep side by side? Body heat will make all of us more comfortable. Eric and Marie can share a set of pews. Livia and Roxanne could sleep together. Sean and I could pair up, as could Allen and Les. It's just an idea, so no one should feel forced to participate."

"I'd rather be where I can check the stove once in a while," Les said. "I won't disturb anyone if I'm by myself."

"I'll stretch out close to you," Allen said, "so you can call if you need help."

But the rest of them agreed that they'd like some extra warmth. When Livia lay back-to-back with Roxanne, she was more comfortable than the night before. Wedged together as the seats were, there wasn't any danger of falling out of bed as she'd done last night.

Although she was physically and mentally tired, Livia's mind was too busy to go to sleep. The pain of being separated from her family during one of the special times of the year was a blow to her. Still, she was pleased to spend this Christmas season with Quinn.

Perhaps she'd read more into his embrace than she should have, but she sensed his feelings toward her in that brief hug went beyond the spiritual regard of one believer to another. If she'd had to choose between being at Heritage Farm tonight or in this abandoned church building with Quinn, which one would she have chosen? She really didn't know. Perhaps God had spared her the choice.

Livia did sleep finally, but her slumbers were fitful. She was aware every time that Les slipped out of his blankets and checked the stove. But she knew that the elderly man slept some because he snored intermittently.

Roxanne was a good sleeping partner, because she seldom moved during the night, and her deep, even breathing, whether asleep or awake, comforted Livia. She woke up when the dawning of the day filtered some light into the building. Her face felt frigid. If Les or Quinn didn't stir the fire soon, she intended to.

Trying not to wake Roxanne, Livia sat up. She peered over the back of the pew and saw Allen sitting up in bed. Les's blankets were empty.

When Allen saw that she was awake, he lifted his hand in greeting. Quinn's head appeared over the top of the pew where he'd spent the night with Sean beside him. He looked toward Livia, and quietly mouthed the words, "Merry Christmas."

"You, too," she whispered back.

Allen walked over to Quinn. Whispering, he said, "Quinn, I'm worried about Les. I woke up an hour ago, and he was gone. I figured he'd gone out for fuel, and I dropped back to sleep. He's still not here. Shouldn't we look for him?"

Chapter Eight

"How long has it been daylight?" Quinn asked, throwing back the blanket and vaulting out of the seat.

"I don't know," Allen answered. "My watch says eight o'clock. I peeked outside, and it feels a lot warmer, but we're fogged in. Kind of a strange weather phenomenon, I think."

Quinn had awakened Sean when he'd gotten up. "What's wrong?" Sean asked.

Quinn explained quietly.

"What are you going to do?" Sean said, yawning and standing up.

"I'm going to find him. It's dangerous for anyone to be out in this weather for very long."

"I'll go with you," Sean said. "I've had all of this church pew I can stand."

"It *would* be safer if two of us go," Quinn said.

"Quinn," Allen protested, "I'll go with Sean. I see you're still favoring that leg."

"It needs to be limbered up," Quinn said. He put on the heavy coat he'd shed before trying to sleep and limped toward the door. After taking a quick glance outside, he said, "Apparently there's a warm front moving in from the south. A man could easily get disoriented in this thick fog. Only two of us should go out at a time. Sean and I can go first. We'll look around in the back first."

"I can do that myself," Sean said, as he shrugged into his fleece-lined coat, zipped it up to cover the lower half of his face and tied the hood securely.

"We should stay together, because we can easily get separated in this fog," Quinn said. "I'll go with you."

"You'd better take a light," Allen said. "And here's a piece of rope that we had left from fixing the bell yesterday. It wouldn't be a bad idea to tie it around your waists. That fog is so thick, you won't be able to see one hand in front of the other."

Believing it was sound advice, Quinn secured the rope around his waist, and handed the other end to Sean. Six feet of rope separated them, allowing them freedom of movement.

They covered the back area where the woodshed and johnny houses were, but they didn't see any sign of Les.

"I don't believe he's been out here," Sean said. "The wind has covered our tracks from last night, and there aren't any new tracks in the snow."

"I agree," Quinn said. "So that means he went out the front door. Fortunately, it's not as cold as it was at midnight, but the temperature is still below freezing. We must find him as soon as possible."

When they went back inside, everyone was up. Marie still sat in the pew she'd shared with her husband, her eyes befuddled with sleep.

"No sign that he's been in the backyard," Quinn reported. "We'll go out front and see what we can find."

"I'll help look, too," Eric volunteered.

Quinn shook his head. "No, only two of us at a time. I can't believe an old-timer like Les would slip away like this. He can't have gone far, but let's do this in shifts. When Sean and I get tired, we'll come back, and you and Allen can go. It might be a good idea for you to ring the church bell every fifteen minutes—that way we can keep our bearings."

Livia walked to the door with them. When she saw the thick fog, she laid her hand on Quinn's shoulder. "Be careful," she said.

He covered her hand with his gloved fingers. "We'll be all right. I just hope that Les is."

All of them had grown fond of Les, and when the door closed behind Quinn and Sean, Eric said, "Let's pray for the safety of all three of them. And then build up the fire so they'll be more comfortable when they bring him back."

He took hold of Marie's and Roxanne's hands. Livia joined hands with Marie and reached for Allen's hand. With only a slight hesitation, he joined their prayer circle.

"Why don't you lead us in prayer, Livia?" Eric said.

"God," Livia prayed, "Your Word teaches that even a sparrow can't fall to the ground unless You are aware of it. We believe You know where Les is, even if we don't. Guide Quinn and Sean as they search for him— lead them in the right direction. Protect them, too, God. Reward them for their willingness to risk themselves for others. For what You have done and what You will do in this situation, we thank You. Amen."

Quinn took the lead when they stepped off the church's steps. They'd gone only a short distance when the building was lost to view. Because the fog hovered about a foot off the ground, it was possible to see where they walked.

"I see footprints in the snow," Sean said.

"Yes, and only one set, so they must be Les's. Looks like he's heading for the vehicles."

"We may be making a mountain out of a molehill. We'll probably find him sitting in his car."

"Let's hope," Quinn answered.

The steps led past the delivery truck and the Westside Community Church van and stopped at Les's car.

"The snow is brushed off the trunk," Sean said. "He must have come down here for something."

Studying the footprints intently, Quinn said, "That's probably true, but where do his tracks go from here? I still can't believe he'd go out alone, when he's been warning us to stay together."

They tramped around in the snow, checked drifts, and peered inside the car, but they didn't find Les.

"Oh, look," Sean said. "We walked over his tracks. He's heading back toward the church."

Giving the younger man a pleased look, Quinn said,

"You may not be a country boy, Sean, but you've got good eyes. That's good tracking. The snow didn't drift in this area between his car and the church van, and our tracks are still there from when we got things yesterday. But I see now, there are fresher tracks that don't have any snow in them at all."

"I'm having a little trouble breathing," Sean said. "This fog is thick, and I seem to take in a mouthful of moist, arctic air every time I say anything."

"Then we'll talk only when necessary."

The tones of the church bell sounded across the snow, and Quinn turned toward the sound, knowing they were heading in the right direction. But when they neared the church, Les's tracks veered off to the right.

"He must have gone into the cemetery," Sean said, and they headed in that direction.

Huge drifts lay throughout the cemetery, but Les had circled most of them. At one place, he'd stumbled into a drift and had crawled out of it. They came to a gravestone, where the snow had been swept away. A bouquet of artificial red poinsettias had been laid at the base of the stone.

The inscription read Ray Holden. The birth and death dates indicated that the boy had died at eighteen.

"Must have been Les's grandson," Quinn commented.

A short distance away, they came to a plot beneath a tall spruce tree close to a woven-wire fence. Again the snow had been brushed away from several Holden stones. A spray of flowers leaned against the marker of Sarah Holden's grave.

"The age would be right for these to be Les's wife and his parents," Quinn said.

Covering his mouth with his hand to keep out the cold air, Sean mumbled, "I suppose he wanted the flowers on their graves for Christmas Day, and preferred to mourn alone. He took a big risk, though."

"He didn't think he could get lost."

The church bell rang again.

Quinn and Sean exchanged worried glances because instead of turning toward the church, Les's steps led through a gap in the fence into a pasture.

"He must have gotten disoriented in the fog," Quinn said. "Are you up to going farther? Or shall we go back, rest up, and send the other guys out?"

Taking a deep breath, Sean said, "We'd better keep going on. If he's down, we need to find him as soon as possible."

The bell rang again, indicating they had walked fifteen more minutes. They found Les face down in a deep drift. He looked lifeless, and Quinn feared to touch him.

Sean turned troubled eyes toward Quinn, who knelt beside Les and touched his face. It was cold, but his body was warm beneath his coat. An erratic pulse beat in the man's forehead. Quinn shook his shoulder, and Les opened his eyes.

"I'm just tuckered out—lost my way in the fog," he mumbled.

Quinn and Sean took his arms and lifted Les to his feet.

"Think you can walk to the church?" Quinn asked.

"Of course I can," Les said, took one step and fell again.

"I'll carry him," Sean said.

"No, I can walk, I tell you," Les said testily in a weak voice. Ignoring his comments, Sean knelt and easily picked him up.

Quinn checked to be sure the rope was still taut between them. "I'll go ahead and break trail," he said. Glancing over his shoulder at Sean, he asked with a slight grin on his face, "Were you a Boy Scout?"

"Yes. For about ten years. I guess it paid off today."

"Put me down, I can walk," Les said querulously, and he grumbled all the way to the church. "Treating me like I was an old man. I don't want to be carried."

"Hush," Sean said. "There comes a time when everyone needs to be carried. Stop squirming around—you're making my work harder."

The bell rang again, and Quinn breathed a silent prayer. They'd almost reached the church. When he could see the building, he called out a greeting, and the door opened immediately. He untied the rope from his waist to give Sean more freedom to carry Les into the building. They entered, and Sean lowered him to a sitting position on a church pew close to the stove.

Roxanne and Livia hurried to Les's side and removed his gloves, checking his fingers for frostbite. They were cold, but not blue.

"What about your feet?" Roxanne said.

"Not much feeling in them," Les admitted.

Allen knelt and removed Les's shoes and socks. Using a blanket they'd been warming, Allen wrapped Les's feet and propped them on a coal bucket so they'd be close to the stove.

"Why did you go out alone?" Allen scolded. "You know better than that. At least, you could have told us where you were going. We've been worried about you."

"If it hadn't warmed up, you could easily have died," Quinn said.

"I know, but I thought I could go out and be back in before any of you woke up. I would have, too, but that fog didn't come until I started into the graveyard. I couldn't see at all for a while, and I just got turned around. My feet's starting to sting, so I may pay for my folly by losing a toe or two."

Examining his feet, Sean said, "I don't think so."

"The water is heated," Allen said, "so you can have a cup of coffee. That should warm you up. Quinn, you and Sean had better have a cup, too."

Taking a swallow of the lukewarm coffee, Quinn said, "That bell really helped us. When neither Sean nor I had been in the cemetery before, we might have gotten lost just like Les. The snow had broken down the fence, and there wasn't anything to warn us not to go into that big pasture."

Eric went for more fuel, and he returned with one bucket of coal.

"I hate to be the bearer of more bad news," he said, "but there's only a few more buckets of coal left, and not a great deal of wood."

"But we'll be all right," Quinn said. "It's getting warmer outside, so we won't freeze although we may be uncomfortable."

His teeth still chattering, Les said, "If we have to, we'll tear down the woodshed and burn it. I can rebuild it as soon as the weather clears up."

Even though Livia didn't like coffee, she drank a cup, merely to have a warm beverage with the dry doughnuts she ate for breakfast. She was beginning to feel hungry now, because they'd not had much to eat for two days.

"Let's plan our Christmas dinner," she said. "Allen, can you think of anything else we can buy from your truck?"

"Preferably something that can be considered holiday food," Roxanne added.

"How about a canned ham?" Allen said. "And there's a case of canned sweet potatoes and some cranberry relish. Do I need to bring more bread? It's probably frozen by now, but I'll go get it."

"Before you go, I've got something to say," Les remarked. "I'm thankful to Quinn and Sean for rescuing me, especially Sean, for I ain't treated him very good."

"Oh, that's no problem," Sean answered easily. "I figured you thought I was a city kid."

"That's part of it. I did think you were a spoiled kid that didn't know much except basketball. But the real reason I didn't cotton to you was because you remind me of my grandson."

Quinn and Sean exchanged glances.

"He died when he was still a teenager, and I guess I kinda resented that you were here and he wasn't. This is the first Christmas without him, and I ain't come to terms with my grievin' yet. The reason I was traveling this way when the storm hit was to put some flowers on his grave. There's a better road to my daughter's house, but I just had a hankering to be with my loved ones that have passed on. I didn't know I'd cause any trouble by going to put the flowers on their graves. So, sonny, I'm sorry I've been mean to you. May the Lord forgive me for it."

Sean closed the distance between them in two long steps. He grasped Les's hands in his. "Don't blame yourself. I didn't make a good first impression because I don't like winter weather, and I was irritated that I couldn't go home."

"While we're in a confessing mood," Allen said, "I need to say something." He stood and walked around the room, and with his back toward them, he said, "Probably you've guessed that I don't have the same faith the rest of you do. I've not had much use for church people, and I wasn't keen on spending this time with you. But you've taught me that I've been wrong. Seeing the way you handled this change in your plans has taught me a thing or two."

Allen turned to face them, his expression serious and confused. "After the rest of you were sleeping last night, I lay awake doing a lot of thinking. I'm bewildered now, and I don't know where I'm going from here, but I do know I want to be like you people. I hope you'll pray for me."

"We're all praying people," Quinn said. "Give us your telephone number, so we can call and check on your spiritual progress to encourage you."

"I'll need all the help I can get."

"As I said last night, God had a purpose for bringing all of us together," Eric commented. "We're beginning to see the reasons. The future will probably tell us more," he added, with a speculative glance between Quinn and Livia.

"Wouldn't this be a good time to open our presents?" Marie said, to spare Livia the embarrassment that reflected in her eyes. "We should do that before we start to fix our food."

"Suits me," Eric said. "I'll do the honors and pass the gifts around. Let's open our gifts by age—oldest ones go first. We know lots of things about each other, so we might as well tell our ages. Is that okay with everyone?"

They soon sorted out their ages, so that Les was the first to open his gift, with Roxanne in second place. As the youngest in the group, Livia wouldn't open her gift until last.

Only two of the packages were professionally wrapped. The others showed the absence of expert handling.

Sorting through the eight gifts, Eric picked up a flat, loosely wrapped gift, which he handed to Les.

"To Les from Sean," he said.

Les threw a smile Sean's way. "As mean as I've been to you, hard to tell what this might be."

"I just wanted to show you I can do something else besides play basketball," Sean said, returning the smile.

"Oh, my," Les said when he tore the paper away. He held up a pen-and-ink drawing of the interior of the Sheltering Arms Church, focusing on the chancel—the way it must have looked in its heyday. The dirt and cracks had been removed from the windows, and the furniture and floor shone as if they were new, giving a splendor to the old building.

"Sonny, I'll treasure this all the days of my life. Thanks."

"Well, mother-in-law," Eric said. "You're next. 'To Roxanne from Lester.'"

Her gift was wrapped in a brown paper bag, and Roxanne took out a carved wooden dog. "So that's what you were making yesterday," Roxanne said. "Thank you so much. It looks like the little terrier I had when I was a child."

"I always did like to whittle," Les said, embarrassed.

"Allen," Eric said, "I had a gift for you—a pair of gloves that I've only worn a few times. But in light of what you've just told us, I'm going to give you something else."

He handed his Bible to Allen. "I've used this Bible for several years, and it's well-marked with my favorite verses. It's something I cherish, but I want you to have it with my blessings."

It seemed odd to see tears brighten Allen's eyes.

As the rest of the thoughtful gifts were passed to the recipients, it was difficult to remember that they were stranded travelers. Goodwill and love filled the old building as a few rays of sunshine brightened the room.

Roxanne had her daughter's name, and she gave her a set of pearls that she'd bought and had wrapped in Detroit. Marie gave Quinn a set of cologne and after-shave lotion that she'd bought for Eric. "Sorry, honey," she said to her husband, as Quinn unwrapped the gift.

Sean appreciated Livia's scarf, and immediately tied it around his neck. "Wish I'd had this when we were on our rescue mission this morning," he said.

Livia received the last gift, and she'd already figured out that Quinn had pulled her name. Her hands moistened as she unwrapped the beautifully wrapped box that had obviously been bought before they'd been stranded. Whose gift was she getting?

The box contained a music box, with a twirling silver angel on top of the revolving base. With trembling hands, she wound the tape, placed the music box on the table and as the angel revolved slowly, the music of "Angels We Have Heard on High" swirled throughout the room.

Meeting Quinn's eyes briefly, Livia said with all the warmth she could muster, which wasn't much, "Thank you. It's a beautiful gift."

She wanted to say, "Did you buy this for the woman you've been dating? Because if you did, I don't want it."

She knew her thoughts were mean-spirited, because others had received gifts bought for someone else. But her heart was still vulnerable where Quinn was concerned, and she was unsure of herself.

And of Quinn's feelings.

Chapter Nine

By humming "Jingle Bells," and moving in time to the music, the stranded travelers created a festive air, as they heated the sweet potatoes on the stove and sliced the cold ham for sandwiches. As a surprise, Allen had brought two pumpkin pies and one cherry pie to top off the meal.

"As good a Christmas meal as I've ever had," Eric said, with an apologetic look toward Roxanne. "When we've eaten with you on Christmas Day, Mom, I've never really been hungry. I was hungry today."

Roxanne laughed at him. "No need for an apology. I agree with you."

They were sitting around, relaxing after the meal, when Quinn stood suddenly. "Do you hear what I hear?"

And Sean broke into the lyrics of a traditional song. "Do you see what I see?"

Quinn shook his head. "No, I'm serious. I hear a tractor."

They all rushed out on the porch as a huge tractor plowed to a noisy stop before the steps. A burly farmer, dressed in a red woolen coat with a knit cap pulled over his ears, jumped down from his enclosed cab.

"I thought there must be somebody stranded over here," he said. "I heard bells ringing in the night and thought Santa's Rudolph had a bell around his neck." He laughed heartily at his joke. "But I got to studying on it this morning, and I told my missus I'd better have a look-see."

The fog had lifted slightly, and he glanced toward the snowbound vehicles. "Looks like you had trouble. Anybody hurt in the accident?"

Recognizing the farmer, Quinn stepped forward.

"Why, Quinn Damron, what are you doing here?" the farmer exclaimed.

Quinn shook hands with him. To his companions, he said, "I've been to Mr. Dunlow's farm several times, doctoring his animals. He lives over near the interstate, so the bell carried a long way."

Briefly, Quinn explained what had happened to them, how they'd taken shelter in the church, and he introduced his companions. Quinn said, "Come inside, if you have time."

"I won't come in, but is there anything I can do for you? You got anything to eat?"

Quinn motioned to the upended truck. "We've had plenty of food, because that's a grocery truck. Depending on how long we'll be here, we may run out of fuel. Are the roads being plowed now?"

"Yes, the interstate is pretty well cleared, and if the sun shines like they're predicting for the afternoon, there will be some thawing."

"Then we can last through the rest of today and tonight," Les said, stepping from behind Allen.

"Hi, there, Lester," Dunlow said. "How'd an old-timer like you get stranded in a snowstorm?"

Les shrugged his shoulders. "The best of us makes mistakes sometime, Dunlow, although in light of the fellowship we've been havin', I'm not sure this was a mistake."

"Well, you do look hale and hearty," Dunlow said. He reached in his tractor and pulled out a chain saw.

"I'll see to it that you're plowed out as soon as possible," the farmer said, "but there's no reason for you to be cold." He motioned to a dead tree along the roadbed, not far from the church. "I'll saw that tree up for you, and you won't run out of fuel."

More optimistic now that they knew rescue was near, they laughed and joked as they followed Dunlow to the tree. He quickly felled the tree and cut it into lengths that would fit the stove. The snowbound travelers carried the wood to the woodshed and several armfuls into the church, singing as they worked. The extra exertion made Livia feel warmer, and she was perspiring before the last chunk of wood was taken inside.

Before Dunlow climbed back on his tractor, he said, "We've been using our telephones right along, and soon's as I get back, I'll report your whereabouts to the state road workers. Do you want me to call your families and tell them you're all right?"

"That would be wonderful!" Livia exclaimed. "Our families don't have any idea where we are, and I get no cell phone reception out here."

"My wife likes to talk on the phone, 'specially now that she's snowbound. You write down the telephone numbers and names. She'll notify your kin."

Livia got her notebook and wrote down the numbers as each one dictated.

"Just one call will do for the three of us," Roxanne said. "I'll give you the name of my sister."

The farmer absolutely refused to take the money they offered him for the long distance calls. "Nope. I'd be a miserly creature if I can't help my fellowmen once in a while without being paid for it."

Dunlow tucked the paper in his coat pocket, climbed back into the tractor cab and shouted above the noise of the engine, "Merry Christmas!"

He waved, and went roaring back the way he'd come. Knowing that their rescue was imminent, the group returned to the church building with a lighter heart.

Despite the warmer weather, when the sun went down, the building was cold, and they again took shifts keeping their sanctuary warm. A lot had changed since Quinn and Livia had sat together two nights ago. Although Livia was anxious to get home, she had mixed feelings about being rescued because she was enjoying her time with Quinn.

Although they'd sat silently for a long period, Quinn must have shared her thoughts, because he said, "Sounds as if this time tomorrow night, we'll be going on to our respective homes," Quinn said. "Livia, it's been wonderful running into you again. Will we continue to see each other now?"

"Do you want to see me?" she asked.

"Well, of course," he said quickly. "I just said I'd enjoyed seeing you again."

"But you're dating someone."

"Yes, but we're really more like friends keeping each other company for dinners and things."

"Did you buy the music box for her?"

His green eyes widened in amazement. "No, I didn't. I bought her a gift, but it wasn't the music box."

"Then who did you buy it for?"

"You."

"Me! You didn't know you'd even see me!"

"No, I didn't know it, but God knew we'd be together for Christmas. I saw the music box in a jewelry store display case when I was shopping in the mall. I thought it was a beautiful thing. I bought it on impulse, not having any idea what I'd do with it. When I met you again and was fortunate enough to choose your name, I was sure the gift was meant for you."

Shamefaced, Livia said, "I'm sorry I jumped to the wrong conclusion. Thinking you'd bought it for someone else, spoiled the gift for me. I'll really treasure it now."

"Since we got started off on the wrong foot once before let's start over. I won't ask for any commitments now, but I'd like to see where this leads. God seems to have thrown us back together for a reason. Will you let me come and visit you at Heritage Farm? After that, I'll have my mother invite you to come to our home. Then if we still enjoy being together, it's an easy trip for me to drive to OSU every other weekend. Does that sound like a good plan to you?"

Livia didn't know why she hesitated. He was offering what she'd wanted for three years. Was she going to be foolish again and drive Quinn away from her forever?

"Yes, it does. I've always wanted you to see Heritage Farm and meet my family. Let's exchange phone numbers, and we'll arrange a weekend visit as soon as possible. I find it hard to forgive myself for the awkwardness of the past and our lost friendship."

He took her hand. "Don't be hard on yourself. I was at fault, too. Let's forget it."

"I'm not sure it's best to forget what happened. We need to learn from our mistakes. I don't want to go through again what I have for the past three years."

"These few days we've been together, and they seem like weeks, I've kept playing the 'What Might Have Been' game, wondering where we'd be today if we hadn't lost track of each other."

She looked at him, amazement on her face. "I've been doing the same thing," she said. "I've wondered if we'd still be seeing each other, or if a few months of dating would have shown us that we aren't compatible at all."

He shook his head. "I don't really believe that would have happened." He pulled her into the shelter of his arm, and kissed her forehead. "I've felt kinda sad when I've noticed how much Eric and Marie love each other, wondering how much I've missed by not continuing to see you."

Livia didn't answer, and he realized she was crying. Tears slowly found their way down her cheeks, and she swiped them away. He didn't think he should ask her why she was crying, but he wrapped his arms around her and rocked her gently back and forth.

Livia yielded to the driving sobs that shook her body as the tears washed away the rejection and unhappiness that had dominated her heart. In Quinn's arms, she put the indecisive period of her past behind her. Someday she would tell Quinn how she felt, but not tonight. All she wanted now was to continue to enjoy the security of his arms.

When she quieted, with a tender hand, Quinn lifted her face. Tears still trembled on her eyelids, and he wiped them away. Quinn's lips caressed hers tenderly until he realized that Livia was responding. His lips were warm and sweet on hers, and Livia knew that today marked a new beginning for them.

After the interlude with Quinn, Livia thought she would sleep, but the pews she occupied with Roxanne seemed harder than the night before. How easy it had been, in Quinn's arms, to put the past behind her and bury the disappointments and embarrassments which had made her miserable for years.

She realized now that her faith had been weak, or she wouldn't have let one bitter incident distress her for so long. Her parents had taught their children from infancy that God had a plan for each individual's life. To find true happiness, one had to submit *personal* will to *God's* will. She hadn't done that. She had made up her mind three years ago that she wanted Quinn, and instead of waiting for God's timing in the matter, she'd planned her own agenda to get him.

Now she fully understood it had been God's will all along for her and Quinn to be together. Considering her immaturity at age seventeen, if she had started dating Quinn, their relationship probably wouldn't have lasted. Eight years difference in age now didn't seem nearly as much as it had been when they'd first met.

What would her parents think when she sprung Quinn on them suddenly? She'd never mentioned him to any of her family, although she'd often wanted to confide in her brother. But her ego had been so wounded that, like an old dog, she had crawled off by herself to lick her wounds. Probably her mother had known all along that something was bothering her youngest daughter, but Hilda Kessler was a wise woman. She'd raised her children to be self-reliant, and she hadn't pried into her daughter's emotional problems.

God, forgive me, for not trusting You to guide my life. I'm grateful that You brought Quinn back into my life. I won't try to outrun You again. You lead the way—I'll be happy to follow.

* * *

Livia sensed a marked difference in the attitude of her companions when she woke up the next morning and stepped stiffly off of the church pew. For one thing, the sun was shining, which seemed to add to their hope that they would be rescued before the day was over.

They grouped around the stove for breakfast, and Marie must have echoed all of their thoughts. As she chewed halfheartedly on a cold doughnut, she said, "I hope the Lord will forgive me for an ungrateful attitude, but once we get out of this predicament, I don't think I'll ever eat another doughnut."

Her comment brought a universal laugh from her companions.

"The same thought was rolling through my mind," Sean said, "but I've complained so much, I decided to keep my mouth shut for once."

"Matter of fact," Les said with a mischievous grin, "I never did like store-bought doughnuts. My missus used to make doughnuts that would melt in your mouth. I'd sure like to take a bite of one of them."

"Please," Sean said, "don't talk about home-cooked food. My mouth had been watering two days for a large slab of turkey, mashed potatoes, bread stuffing and hot rolls. Lead me to it." He rubbed his stomach and groaned.

"Don't forget about the rest of basketball season," Eric warned. "If you gain a lot of weight, the coach will keep you sitting on the bench."

"You can't gain a pound by dreaming," Sean retorted. "Besides, by the time I get home, my family will be tired of turkey and dressing and will probably be eating pizza."

"That's another no-no word," Quinn protested. "I've been so hungry for a slice of pizza that I even dreamed about eating some last night." Swallowing the last bite of doughnut, he stood. "I'm going to take the broom from the supply room and sweep the snow off of my truck. That way, the sun won't have so much to melt. I'll sweep yours off, Les."

"Thanks," Les said, "but hadn't you better stay off that sore leg."

"I'm having very little trouble with it. I think it was only a pulled muscle."

"I'm convinced that we'll be plowed out today," Roxanne said, "so we need to straighten up this room. Les, can you tell us where everything is supposed to be?"

"Sure. I'll give you a hand on moving the pews back in place."

"I'll take the candles out of the windows and put them back in the supply room." Livia said. "What should we do with the greenery we brought in?"

"There's a place in the back where we burn trash, so I'll pile the branches beside the woodshed. When the snow melts, I'll get rid of the trash."

Marie picked up all the empty cartons, water bottles and other trash—enough to fill two large garbage bags. "We'll put those in my trunk," Les said. "I'll take them to my daughter's—she has garbage removal service."

By ten o'clock, Sean, who had been outside, threw the door wide open.

"Here comes the snowplow. Listen to the engine—that's more beautiful than Handel's 'Messiah,' to my ears right now."

They collided with each other in their haste to hurry outdoors. When the snowplow opened a road to their stranded vehicles, they gave a great shout of welcome.

"Hey," Sean said, "you guys should come to my basketball games. You're making more noise than the fans do when I make a jump shot and win the ball game."

The driver of the snowplow turned the vehicle before he stopped and jumped down from the cab. The men crowded around him, shaking his hand, pounding him on the back. He was bundled against the cold and a heavy beard covered his face. Only his eyes peered out from his woolen stocking cap.

"We're really glad to see you," Quinn said.

"Had a rough time of it, have you?" the man said sympathetically in a kind drawl.

"Not as bad as it could have been," Quinn answered. "We've had food and drinks, as well as a place of shelter."

"How are the highways?" Eric asked.

"The interstate has been plowed, but it's slick in spots. Most of the secondary roads are still covered with snow. We're trying to rescue stranded motorists. Which way are you heading?"

"To Columbus," Eric said.

"You might be better off to take I-65 to Dayton and go east on I-70. That will add distance to your trip, but Highway 23 probably has snow cover in spots. The interstates are safer. The blizzard swept northeast toward the Great Lakes, where some places have two feet of snow. There's only a few inches of snow in Columbus."

"Three of us live locally," Quinn said, "so we can find our way home now that you've plowed the roads."

The plowman walked to the delivery truck. "I can't do much for you," he said to Allen, "except call a wrecker. I'll have one sent as soon as possible. If the rest of you want to follow me as I leave, I'll be handy in case you have any more trouble, which I don't think you will."

"Oh, we don't want to leave Allen behind," Roxanne said.

"You go on your way," Les said. "I ain't in a hurry. I'll stay until they've pulled the truck out."

"I'm not leaving, either," Quinn said. Turning to Allen, he continued, "You'll need a ride to your home after they right the truck. I doubt you should try to drive it until a mechanic checks out the damage. I'll take you home. Those of you going to Columbus can follow the snowplow, since you have the farthest to go."

The eight of them had bonded so quickly during their brief time together that it was like leaving old friends to say goodbye. With helpful directions from Quinn, Eric turned the van around on the narrow road, while Sean and the women went into the church for their luggage.

When he saw that the other church passengers were storing their gear in the van, Quinn realized that Livia was in the church alone. He stepped inside just as she picked up her luggage.

"Will you leave for home as soon as you return to Columbus?"

"Yes. I already have my things packed. I'll go as soon as possible."

"For how long?"

"It will be two weeks before I return to OSU."

"I'd like to see you before then."

"Call me at home," Livia said. She gave him her cell phone number, as well as the house number at Heritage Farm. "Unless it interferes with plans my folks have already made, would you want to come for New Year's weekend?"

"I'd love to. I'll be in touch in a few days."

He didn't want to delay her companions, but Quinn needed the reassurance that Livia had a place in his future. He opened his arms wide, and she rushed inside. It was too soon to say, "I love you," but Quinn knew that his heart had found a lodging place in the woman he gathered close.

Livia's heart lurched with happiness, knowing that the love of her life was within her grasp. She felt like that breathless girl of seventeen who'd fallen so completely for Quinn. She put her arms around his neck and lifted her face for his kiss. Livia's eyes closed as their lips touched, filling her heart with warmth and peace.

By noon the next day, Livia turned her small car into the curved driveway that led to Heritage Farm. The Kesslers had settled this land prior to the Civil War, and the brick house, now painted white, had been built a few years later. The magnificent house was situated on a rounded knoll that overlooked the Ohio River.

Livia's foot pressed on the gas pedal as she climbed the hill. Home had never looked so good! When she brought her car to a halt at the rear of the original house, the door opened, and her mother stepped out.

Hilda Kessler's blond hair was streaked with gray, but her blue eyes gleamed serenely. Livia couldn't remember a time when she'd been away for any length of time that Hilda hadn't been standing in that door to welcome her home.

Turning off the ignition, Livia jumped out of the car and ran to her mother.

"I've been thanking God for keeping you safe. It's good to have you home," Hilda said in her soft voice. "We've missed you."

"Oh, Mom, it's been the most incredible experience I've ever had! I can't wait to tell you all about it."

On the last day of the year, Livia stood at that same door and watched Quinn's truck turn off the highway into her family's private driveway. It pleased her that all of the Christmas guests were gone, and that her parents were on an errand into town. A few days of absence made her somewhat unsure of Quinn's feelings for her, and she preferred to be alone when she saw him again.

When he stopped the truck, Livia walked toward him, her hands outstretched. "Welcome to Heritage Farm."

Quinn kissed her gently on the cheek. "I've missed you, Livia."

"Yes, when our group spent three days together, it seemed unusual not to look around and see you or one of the other six. Come inside."

Quinn took a minute to survey the broad fertile fields located along the Ohio River with the appreciative eyes of a farmer.

"This is a beautiful farm. I can see why it means so much to your family."

She led him into the large, cozy family room. "Mom and Daddy had to be away for the afternoon." With a sheepish grin, she said, "Actually, I think it was a contrived errand to give us a little time to ourselves. My immediate family will all be here for supper."

"I look forward to meeting your folks, but I wanted to see you alone first. Have you told your parents about us?"

"Not everything, but I did fill them in on our meeting at camp a few years ago. I hesitated to say too much—I was afraid that our emotions may have been overworked when we were stranded together. I thought I'd better be sure you hadn't changed your mind before I said anything."

"I had to explain to my parents why I was making this visit, but I couldn't go into any details. I know I said that we'd take some time before we made any decisions, but I don't have any doubt. I've made up my mind—I want to marry you, Livia."

"Is that a proposal?" she said, her heart fluttering at his words.

He grinned sheepishly. "Yes, but not a very romantic one, I guess. It sounded more like a demand than a proposal. So let me start over. I love you, Livia, and if you can find it in your heart to love me, too, we ought to get married."

Her eyes glistened mischievously, and he laughed aloud. "That's even worse than my first attempt," he said.

Livia laughed with him. "Why don't you propose like my grandfather did? When he met my grandmother, he knew right away that she was the one for him. A week later, he went to her house. When she came to the door, he said, 'Let's get hitched.' That seemed to work. They were together for over fifty years."

"Do you want to?" he asked.

"Want to what?"

"Get hitched?"

Smothering a laugh, Livia said, "Yes."

Hearing a car approaching the house, Quinn guessed her parents were returning. He had hoped for more time alone with her before he met the others, but taking advantage of the situation, Quinn pulled Livia into a bear hug.

"Then that's all I need to know," he said. "We'll work out the details later."

They were still kissing when Livia heard the outside door open. She broke the embrace and looked quickly toward her parents as they stood in the doorway. She frantically tried to think of an explanation until she noted the expressions on their faces. Karl and Hilda Kessler didn't seem at all surprised to see the tall, dark-haired man kissing their youngest daughter.

Epilogue

A balmy breeze blew across the area, but the sun was shining as Quinn and Livia turned off the interstate and took the secondary road to Sheltering Arms Church. After they'd been married three years ago, Livia and Quinn had set up their veterinarian practice in Bowling Green. Livia took care of the small-animal end of the business, while Quinn devoted his time to farm stock.

Since they lived nearby, they'd often driven by the church where they'd been reunited five years ago. But today they'd come for a reunion with the travelers with whom they'd shared three anxiety-filled yet exhilarating days. The snowstorm that stranded the eight of them at Sheltering Arms Church had gone down in the history books as one of the worst blizzards in northwestern Ohio.

Turning in her seat to be sure that six-month-old

Ruth was still cozy in her car seat, Livia said to her husband, "Quinn, I'm so excited. Won't it be wonderful to see everyone again?"

"Sure will. I feel like we're going to a family reunion."

"I feel closer to these people than some of my own relatives, so it *is* a family reunion. I'm a little sad though that Les won't be with us."

"Yes, but he left his mark on the old church. I'm sure we'll be aware of his presence."

Six months ago, Quinn and Livia had attended Les's funeral in the church. Livia looked toward his grave marker as Quinn parked their van.

Annie Colver, Les's daughter, who'd taken on the role of looking after the church since her father's death, came out to greet them.

Livia carried Ruth's car seat into the church, while Quinn brought in two picnic baskets.

"I've pushed the seats forward and put up these folding tables in the back to hold our food," Annie said. "We won't need much heat tonight, but I built a fire in the stove to remind you of your wintery sojourn here."

The next to arrive were Roxanne, Marie and Eric, who led their two-year-old son into the building. Eric was now the senior pastor of a church in Illinois, and the Damrons hadn't seen the Stover family since Livia had graduated from OSU.

Soon after their forced stay at Sheltering Arms Church, Allen Reynolds had moved to the Cincinnati area. Quinn had kept in touch with Allen as a spiritual mentor, and they looked forward to meeting his wife and two daughters.

Sean was the last to arrive, and his friends cheered as he drove up in his late-model Jaguar. With his first check from his NBA contract, Sean had bought Sheltering Arms Church from the denomination that owned it and established a trust fund for the permanent upkeep of the building and cemetery. He had invested stewardship of the property in a board of local citizens with the stipulation that the original architecture of the building be maintained.

The windows had been repaired and the walls painted and papered. The exterior of the building had been repaired and painted, and the sign refurbished.

As they took a tour of the premises, the friends noticed that the woodshed and the johnny houses had new roofs. Otherwise, the area seemed unchanged.

Livia shivered and, pointing to the johnny houses, she whispered to Marie, "I can still feel the cold air and blowing snow we had to endure to make our trips to this building."

"Yes," Marie agreed. "But it doesn't look like it will snow tonight."

Motioning to the sun setting in a clear sky, Livia said, "I don't think there's any danger of that."

They gathered around the two folding tables Annie had provided, filled with turkey and ham, vegetables, salads and desserts. Marie had brought two dozen doughnuts as a comical reminder of how many of them they'd eaten when they were snowbound. As they enjoyed the food, their conversation centered nostalgically on the past.

Electricity was still not available in the building, so Annie lit candles as dusk fell. When Roxanne started playing the piano, now in tune and melodious, the others took their seats.

Sitting in the pew beside Quinn, holding Ruth in her arms, Livia reflected on the past five years. She and Quinn had been engaged two years before they were married, giving her time to finish college. Their marriage had been the love match she'd always dreamed of having. And the thing that made it so special was their mutual commitment to the Lord's service.

Eric stood behind the lectern and read the Scripture he'd used for his text five years ago. "'But when the fullness of the time was come, God sent forth His Son.'"

Livia was thankful that God had worked His will in her life at the right time. She had wanted to be with Quinn when she'd met him as a teenager. But it wasn't God's timing. She'd often wondered if they had been married when she was so immature, if their marriage could have survived.

A sob filled her throat when Livia thought how blessed she was tonight. She lifted her hand and caressed Quinn's face. He shifted his eyes from Eric to look at her. He took her hand and kissed the palm, then he bent over and pressed a light kiss on her lips. Marveling at the love she felt for him, Livia realized that they were sitting in the same pew where he'd kissed her for the first time.

Quinn continued to hold her hand as Sean stood to sing "O Little Town of Bethlehem." The words found lodging in Livia's heart as if she were hearing them for the first time.

"No ear may hear His coming, but, in this world of sin, where meek souls will receive Him still, the dear Christ enters in."

Livia bowed her head and worshiped the Child in the manger who'd become the Savior of all mankind.

* * * * *

Dear Reader,

In every life, there comes a time when we need a refuge, a shelter in the time of storm. Christians have that refuge/shelter in the Holy Spirit, who dwells in our hearts. As you read my story of eight stranded people, perhaps you've already found a refuge in our Lord, Jesus Christ. If not, I pray that the message of the book will find lodging in your heart, and that you will seek a security to strengthen your faith through bad and/or good times.

It has been a pleasure to share this second book with Dana Corbit. We count it a privilege and blessing to have produced these stories for your reading pleasure. Thanks to the Steeple Hill editors for giving us the opportunity.

Irene B. Brand

A SEASON OF HOPE

Dana Corbit

* * *

To my dear friends Maija Anderson, Toni Brock,
Joy Golicz, LuAnn Taylor and the two Melissas—
M. Baxter and M. Lucken. I have been so privileged
to know real, amazing women like all of you. I'm
blessed to call you friends. Thank you for always
believing in me and in my stories. My life and
those stories are richer because of you.

It is not for you to know the times or the seasons,
which the Father has put in His own power.
—*Acts* 1:7

Chapter One

The world was filled with two kinds of people as far as David Wright was concerned. In the first group were the lucky jokers who actually learned from their mistakes. Those in the second group were doomed to repeat theirs with the regularity of a three-legged dog addicted to traffic hopscotch.

David would have preferred to include himself in the first group since rehabilitation was a cornerstone in his line of work. But as he stared down at the flared sleeves of his scratchy robe and rubbed at the itchy adhesive securing his grizzled beard, he saw the evidence that he was a card-carrying member of the group that never learned.

"David, are you ready?" Martin Rich called as he stuck his head inside the men's room door at New Hope Church.

"Be right out."

Bustling sounds filtered through the open door, carrying a whistled version of "I'll Be Home for Christmas." Obviously, somebody was a lot happier than he was spending the last two days before Christmas in Destiny, Indiana, taking a fictional journey from Nazareth to Judaea. He wished Martin would close the door and shut out the holiday spirit. He wasn't in the mood for it.

Instead, the lanky middle-aged banker stepped inside. In a Wise Man getup rather than one of his tailor-made suits, Martin looked as ridiculous as David did, though the older man seemed blissfully unaware of it.

"Here, let me help." Before David had time to resist, Martin had stuffed an ugly striped hat on his head. "Now that really *tops* off the costume."

David ignored the bad pun as he frowned into the mirror. "Gee, thanks."

"No problem." Martin paused to adjust his own Bethlehem-chic chapeau. "Destiny's second annual live nativity scene would be a bust without you. If not for Joseph, who would get Mary to the inn on time?"

David shrugged. Who indeed? And he wasn't talking about the Biblical story, either. No one else would have been gullible enough to be coerced into wearing this robe not once, but twice. He should have known better after last year's performance, when an abandoned baby girl was discovered in the manger and chaos erupted. But he hadn't *known better,* and now if the last-minute cast replacement was the worst thing to happen, he would consider himself blessed.

Martin pulled the door open again but looked back over his shoulder. "She got to you, too, didn't she?"

David nodded, not bothering to ask who the *she* was when they both knew how persuasive Allison Hensley—now Chandler—could be when she set her mind to something. As her best friend, David hadn't stood a chance against those puppy dog eyes.

"She had this big idea that I should reprise my role as Joseph to her Mary." And he'd given in, knowing full well what a farce it was for him to play a member of the Holy Family when Allison was his only connection to the church these days.

"She pulled one over on you then."

It sure felt like she had, though in his heart, David knew she never would have intentionally bailed on him. Besides, no one became that sick on purpose. He would have defended his friend's honor if Martin's hearty laughter hadn't suddenly filled the room. It sounded so much like the cartoon version of the Jolly Old Elf that David was tempted to say, "Wrong story, bud."

But because the whole situation was a mess, he added a little Charles Dickens to the mix. "Bah. Humbug!"

He felt more like Ebenezer Scrooge than the Christ child's earthly father anyway, and dreaded the rehearsal, the performance and the introduction to the stand-in Mary. Especially that. Though the Biblical Joseph probably had plenty on his mind, such as the heavy responsibility of parenting God's son, David figured that at least he hadn't had to worry that the stable scene was part of a friend's matchmaking scheme.

Already, David could use his dating honor roll to paper the walls of the refurbished warehouse he called home. After four years of playing the field since law school, even he was getting sick of himself. So why did his friend insist on trying to set him up with another woman—especially her twenty-five-year-old cousin?

A pang of guilt struck him for the self-centered jerk he was. Allison was probably too busy chasing after her adopted year-old daughter and suffering bouts of morning, noon and night sickness with her problem pregnancy to make his love life her top priority. She'd only asked her cousin to fill in because she was too sick to get out of bed.

"Yo, David, are you with me?" Martin called out. "Quit daydreaming so we can get this rehearsal over before New Year's."

As David slumped after him out the church door, the frigid east-central Indiana wind and the farm stench from hay and livestock bombarded his senses. Even with the long underwear he'd remembered this time, the wind clawed at his clothes and invaded his bones. His ears and fingers already ached, and his cheeks burned. If it was this cold under the steel gray helmet of daylight, he wondered what it would be like after dark.

"Have you met our new Mary?" Martin asked as they crossed the field toward the makeshift stable.

"Not yet."

"Then now's as good a time as any. Hey, Sondra."

Guessing that this time was no *worse* than any other, David glanced at the woman whose head came up when she heard her name. Even if she hadn't strode toward them, her costume would have given her away.

Instead of waiting for Martin to introduce them, she shot out her hand in a practiced businesslike manner. "Hi. I'm Sondra Stevens."

"David Wright."

She had a firm handshake despite her fingers being so icy cold that they must have felt numb. He tried to ignore the tickle in his palm when he released her.

"You might recognize David's name from the political signs outnumbering Christmas lights this year." Martin chuckled. "If he wins next month's special election, at twenty-eight he'll be the youngest Superior Court judge in Cox County history."

"That's quite an accomplishment," she said.

Funny, the bank teller he'd had dinner with last week had appeared more impressed when he'd shared that news with her.

"Sondra is the assistant human resources director at Tool Around, Kentucky's largest RV manufacturer. She's on her way up in that company."

His introduction duties finished, Martin excused himself to join the other Wise Men. David didn't like the strange feeling that he'd been left to fend for himself as he turned back to Sondra.

From beneath the costume's head covering, huge mahogany-hued eyes stared out at him. Those eyes trapped him under their intelligent and evaluating gaze, making him wonder if Sondra was in the habit of studying others to determine their worthiness for her attention. That she looked away and readjusted her shawl clued him in that she'd found him lacking. On some elemental level, it bothered him that she could dismiss him so easily.

"I'm playing Joseph," he said needlessly.

Laughter lit her eyes, but it stopped at her mouth. "I figured it was that or you had interesting taste in clothing."

"I have great taste in clothes…and everything else." Why he'd said it David wasn't sure, other than that he'd felt a sudden need to defend himself.

"So I've heard."

"My reputation precedes me."

Most days it didn't bother him to have a reputation as the local bachelor attorney who'd dated most of Destiny's single women—none more than twice. Since he'd long ago accepted that he wasn't cut out for the deep stuff, he'd always been decent to his dates, keeping things casual so nobody got hurt. It was strange, but today he wished the reputation didn't follow him so closely, ruining his chance for a good first impression.

"Yes, it does. Impressive."

Her tone suggested she wasn't really impressed by whatever she'd heard. She paused long enough to make him squirm, if he were the type to shift under cross-examination. He wasn't.

"Allison said you made a good Joseph." She lifted an eyebrow and lowered it.

"Touché." He smiled, letting her have her joke and resisting the urge to wonder what she'd really been hint-ing at before. "If I know Allison at all, she probably said my performance was fabulous or stupendous."

"Something like that, but I like to stick to the facts and forget the flowery words. Allison and I are opposites that way."

She had that right. Even having just met her, he sensed that the two of them were different in a lot of ways. They wore the same blue costume and both had oval-shaped faces, but that was all they appeared to have in common.

Allison was the perfect woman to play Jesus' mother. A nurturer, the former social worker was so kind and warm that she drew people the way flowers turned to sunshine. Sondra, on the other hand, was an unlikely Mary. She seemed tough and arrogant instead of submissive to God's will, the way Jesus' mother had been.

Even in appearance, Sondra was as dark as Allison was light. Allison's blond tresses streamed down her back, while her cousin cut her nearly black hair short in a no-nonsense style. His friend had always fought the height-weight battle, but Sondra was willowy and so tall her costume only brushed her ankles.

She was also tall enough to nearly look a man in the eye, particularly one like him who lacked two inches to reach six feet. And any man wouldn't have had a tough time looking back at the exotic beauty, with her flawless light bronze skin and sculpted features.

He was already admiring her eyelashes, that never in a million years would require mascara, when she drew her eyebrows together as a huge clue that he'd been staring.

David cleared his throat. "Uh, thanks for filling in at the last minute. Not that anyone can fill Allison's shoes completely. She came up with this whole idea last year and pulled it together."

"I'm not trying to fill her shoes, but I did want to be here for her. Allison needed me."

She might as well have tossed a bucket of water over him, as effectively as her comment woke him up. What was he thinking, noticing any woman right now, especially Allison's cousin? Didn't he have enough on his plate with an election to win, messed-up priorities to get in order and a sick puppy of a friend to help out?

That was another thing. If Allison needed anyone right now, she needed *him*. Okay, she just might need Cox County Sheriff's Deputy Brock Chandler, too. Brock was, after all, her husband. But if Allison needed a friend, David had already dug in the trenches and was ready for battle. He didn't need any reinforcements from Allison's Kentucky relatives.

Sondra rubbed her hands together. "It's freezing out here."

"That's Indiana for you. They're predicting four to six inches of snow before Christmas morning."

"Too bad I won't be around long enough to see it."

She sure didn't sound disappointed about missing Indiana's white Christmas. He got the idea that she wanted to see Destiny in her rearview mirror as quickly as possible. That was a good thing. He would be more than happy to help her to her car.

"I couldn't believe it when Allison called me," she

said, breaking the silence that had stretched too long. "I've never heard of a pregnant woman being so sick that she had to have a portable IV."

"The doctors call it hyperemesis, which means that she threw up a lot. Constantly, in fact. Finally, the nurse put in a PIC line—or percutaneous invasive catheter—to fight dehydration. You probably aren't aware of this, but in the first twelve weeks of her pregnancy, she's lost ten pounds instead of gaining any weight."

He took smug satisfaction in the shock registering on Sondra's face. She didn't know about Allison's condition or any of the fancy medical terms that he could spout now. She hadn't been there. He had.

"If only she'd called…" She let her voice trail off, her regret unmistakable.

He had poised his hand to squeeze her shoulder in comfort before he realized what he was doing. It wasn't his business. This case wasn't his to judge, even if the cousins weren't as close as Sondra wanted him to believe.

Having turned away to collect her pillow from a nearby haystack, Sondra fortunately missed his lapse. When she turned back, though, her shoulders were straight, as if she'd overcome her own weak moment.

"But as she said, 'The show must go on.'" She rested her hands on a pillow stomach that looked more like she'd swallowed a basketball than she carried a baby inside.

"Do you think they need us over there yet?"

"You know the story, don't you? Joseph and Mary arrive late, when all of the rooms in the inn are full."

"I know the story."

He shrugged. "We do need to get over to the donkey, though."

"That donkey?" She pointed to the Shetland pony someone was leading across the grass.

"That's the one."

"We really are doing some acting here."

The corners of his mouth pulled up. "Stella has the toughest role. She's doing a pony encore performance."

David decided he needed to focus on his own encore. Whenever he'd needed Allison, she'd dropped everything for him. She'd never asked much of him in return. Well, she was relying on him this one time to make the show go off without any more hitches. She needed him to do this, and he wouldn't let her down.

Leading Sondra across the churchyard to the mark for their theatrical entry into Bethlehem, David couldn't resist shooting a glance back at the wooden stable. As long as the child in the manger remained a doll, they could handle anything.

Chapter Two

Sondra settled herself sidesaddle on their "donkey" and wondered where her life had taken the wrong turn that had landed her in this place. It must have been the moment she took the ramp onto Interstate 65, heading north to Indiana. Or well before it, when, during a moment of weakness, she'd agreed to participate in Allison's harebrained plan.

Who was she kidding? She would have done almost anything for her cousin whom, along with Aunt Mary and Uncle Bruce, she owed for all the normal experiences of her childhood. Every trip to Indiana Beach or Brown County State Park came as a backseat passenger in the Hensleys' car. She was indebted to them for so much more—for freely given hugs and for little-girl trinkets her single mom couldn't afford—but working with David Wright was stretching the limits of her gratitude.

The least she could expect was a little appreciation for her dropping everything, crossing a state line and driving past acre after acre of flat, Hoosier farmland to reach Destiny. But David didn't even give her credit for her trouble. In fact, he seemed to resent her for just being there. What did he plan to do, play Mary and Joseph all by himself? Maybe he could crawl into the manger and play the Baby Jesus while he was at it.

Sondra couldn't help smiling at the image of big strong David curled up in the hay. Or sporting her costume and pillow belly for that matter.

A disloyal part of her figured it would be a waste for him to hide all his dark wavy hair beneath her heavy head shawl. Even with his hair clipped short on the sides, he couldn't hide its tendency to curl. If David wore her strange costume, the blue robe would only accentuate his light blue eyes. Translucent eyes that seemed to see everything yet reveal nothing.

Not that she'd noticed or anything. Or if she had noticed, she hadn't wasted any time dwelling on what she'd seen. Or if she had dwelled just a bit, then she at least was too smart to let a pretty face turn her head.

That the pony chose this moment to whinny and flip its mane, forcing her to tighten her grip on the reins, only annoyed her. David certainly wasn't harboring any attraction for her; he'd made that clear enough with the way he'd treated her. And from what her cousin had told her about him, he wasn't especially selective in choosing his many dating partners. What did it say about her that the skin on her arms tingled just because of David's nearness as he stood next to the pony? She wasn't that desperate for dates. Maybe long-term relationships weren't her thing, but she'd had her share of dinners and movies.

Again, Stella whinnied and stomped her foot.

David glanced over and frowned. "You're not going to lose control, are you? We don't need you galloping into Bethlehem tonight like a bad cowboy wanna-be."

Sondra narrowed her gaze at him and patted the pony's neck. She crooned to the horse instead of speaking to him. "Don't you listen to that old grouch, Stella. You and I know you'll pull this off like an old pro."

She looked at David. "I'm from Louisville, remember? I know how to sit a horse." Okay, she hadn't ridden more than a half-dozen times in her life, but she could ride, and that was all he needed to know.

"Glad to hear it. Wouldn't want the show to turn into a media event like last year." His smile was smug enough to make her fist her fingers over the reins. The teeth he flashed were straight and white, a fact that only annoyed her further. How could she find a man like him attractive?

"There won't be a problem from me, but I can't speak for anyone else." She raised both eyebrows.

He only kept smiling and continued his habit of grating on her nerves. For someone she'd known less than a half hour, he sure was a quick study at it.

Why did she let him get to her? And why couldn't she resist baiting him in return? She could answer those questions no more than she could figure out why she was so determined to prove herself to him. On her own turf at the office, she no longer had to prove anything to anyone. No one could match her sixty-hour workweeks and the sacrifice of her already limited social life. Now her dream job was within her grasp—human resources director—if only she continued to keep up the pace.

"That's our cue," David told her as the last strains of "O Holy Night" filtered through the sound system. "We might as well get this over with."

He had that right. She needed only to get through this one day and she would fulfill her promise to Allison. Then she would sprint to her car and be across the Indiana-Kentucky border before the first snowflakes fell.

Still, her annoying co-star was just one of the reasons that she wanted her immediate destiny to be far away from Destiny. Just as she remembered from her childhood visits, Destiny seemed to close in around her, trapping her in its suffocating neighborliness.

Give her a big city any day. She'd been gone from Louisville less than a day, and yet she longed for her impersonal apartment in its impersonal complex in an impersonal area just outside the city. At least she figured missing home was what had caused the dull ache inside her as she'd passed by some of Center Street's tiny, holiday-decorated homes. People inside them were probably peeking out their shades as she drove by, picking her out for the stranger she was.

How people could survive in such a small town where everyone knew each other's business, she couldn't imagine. Two-bit towns like this one were where some women ended up when they gave up their dreams for a man. Others just became lonely, bitter women like her mother. She would never repeat her mother's mistakes.

Because the only way out of Destiny was to get this rehearsal and the final performance over with, Sondra reluctantly handed David her pony's reins and let him lead her onto the set. Letting a guy lead her anywhere, now that was a first—and last if she had anything to say about it. At least this was only theater.

"This is the life, isn't it?" David said softly as they neared the stable. "Just a man taking care of his little family."

Sondra had to grip the saddle horn to keep from hopping down and tackling him. Worse than his guessing she would be uncomfortable letting a man take her horse's reins, David seemed to enjoy her discomfort.

"It took a special man to be the adoptive father of Jesus," she whispered back. "Most men couldn't have handled the job."

She couldn't resist stressing the words "most men" or including him in that category, because David Wright was a jerk with a capital "J." If she did an Internet search for the word "jerk," his picture and resume would probably appear as top match. She couldn't believe Allison had offered last year to set her up with him. Didn't her cousin like her at all?

Well, she refused to let him bother her any longer. She wouldn't let his rudeness get to her, and she wouldn't allow herself to be affected by his good looks. She'd promised Allison, and that's all there was too it. She wasn't like her father; she kept her commitments.

Unlike him, she didn't escape in a big rig when the times got tough, leaving the people he allegedly loved in a cloud of diesel exhaust.

No, she wasn't leaving, so David could just forget about pushing her buttons. She would get through this night if it killed her. Or him. Or maybe the both of them.

David yanked the poufy hat off his head and rubbed his frozen ears as he trudged over to his car. If his ears were frostbitten and were amputated, would he still be able to hear cases from the bench? Chances were he'd still be able to hear claims from the prosecution and pleas from the defense, but he would sure look funny doing it.

Settling behind the wheel of Reba, his seasoned sedan with rust-pattern detailing, he turned the key and blasted the heat. Usually he would have taken time to appreciate how the old gal's engine whined and then purred, but then he wasn't usually so rankled with himself.

At the thump of something beating the window, he jerked his head. Martin stood in the wind yelling something outside the glass. If only David had not given Reba a chance to warm up and had driven right off the lot, he could have avoided facing anyone from the cast, but now he was stuck. He cranked open the window.

Martin reached in to pat David's shoulder with his gloved hand. "Well done, young man. Everyone felt the true meaning of Christmas right down to their toes."

"They probably couldn't feel their toes. I know I can't."

Martin demonstrated his full-belly laugh again and nodded. "Okay, maybe a few had frostbitten toes. But if they were watching and listening at all, they also got hearts shock full of praise tonight. You and Sondra did a great job, particularly under such short notice."

David lifted a shoulder and let it fall.

The side of Martin's mouth came up. "That's exactly what Sondra did when I said it to her."

Martin glanced out at the nearly empty field they'd used as a parking lot. "She's probably close to Indianapolis as quickly as she left after the show. Can't say as I blame her. She had a long drive back to Louisville. But it's too bad she couldn't spend the holidays with her cousin."

"That is too bad," David conceded.

Allison probably would have liked that since she no longer had any extended family around. It would have been special to her since it was the first Christmas for Allison and Brock since they'd married and Joy's adoption had become final. Since they'd become a real family. But he'd heard Sondra himself—nothing could have kept her in town.

"Anyway, I'm sure Allison is proud of you, David. You really came through for her."

David swallowed hard, somehow still managing to nod before the Wise Man left to return to his banker's life. If David's actions could be called coming through for Allison, then he wondered to what extremes he would have to go to fail her.

Though the performance had been nearly flawless—

if less exciting than last year's chaos—he couldn't take credit for it. He'd done as much to sabotage the show as any of the other performers had done to make it work.

None of the cast or the audience had frozen to death, the livestock hadn't bit anyone or stampeded, and the sound system had managed not to pick up signals from local baby monitors. Best of all, though, the child in the manger stayed plastic and kept quiet during the whole performance.

Despite him, rather because of him, the show had been serene and worshipful. It spoke to everyone there. For a few seconds, it had even affected him, and nothing spiritual had touched him in years. The event had reminded him of his childhood, when all of this—the star, the shepherds, the manger and its heralded occupant—had really meant something.

Fortunately, only the animals had been close enough to see the dramatic subplot that had unfolded right on stage. From up close, audience members would have recognized that the character Mary never met her husband's gaze during the whole performance, and though her shoulders were curved in submission and praise, her hands were fisted.

David knew because he kept looking over at her, hoping to catch her eye and whisper an apology. She didn't give him the chance. Not that he'd deserved one. He'd tested her patience all afternoon.

But she'd pushed him, too. Every word out of her mouth hinted that she didn't think he was good enough for her, whether she came right out and said it or not.

He should have been pleased that she was every bit as disinterested in him as he was in her and yet he'd found her aloofness unsettling.

None of that mattered. He still doubted Allison would be proud of him for any of this. Ashamed—that was a better word. He was ashamed enough for the both of them. He sure hadn't gained any votes by his behavior tonight.

First thing in the morning, he would call Allison to apologize. He would even offer to write a letter to Sondra and apologize to her, too. If he were fortunate, when he threw himself on her mercy, Allison would volunteer to tell Sondra how sorry he was.

He had it in his favor that his best friend was always gracious in accepting apologies. He'd been on the receiving end of her forgiveness enough to know. But this time he probably would have to count on the fact that it would be Christmas Eve when he faced her. He knew, at least he hoped, that no one could stay angry over Christmas.

Chapter Three

David had to ring the doorbell three times before anyone answered, but the moment the door swung open, he knew why he'd been asked to apologize in person. Been set up was more like it.

"Good morning, David." Sondra's greeting sounded forced, but she still wore a victorious smile.

She looked fresh and comfortable in a yellow sweater and jeans, with her short hair tucked behind her ears. Fuzzy slippers covered her feet, suggesting she wasn't on her way out the door.

Surprise must have thrown him off, but for a fleeting second, David couldn't decide whether to give her a nasty look or grab her and kiss her. Fortunately for him, he did neither. "Hello."

"Hey you guys, catch her, will you?" Allison called from the other room.

As if on cue, a munchkin with a mess of dark curls toddled through Sondra's legs and shot for the door.

David whisked the baby into his arms before the bottoms of her footed pajamas got wet.

"And where do you think you're going, sweetie pea? And where did you get that?" A shaggy teddy bear he'd never seen before dangled from her hand. The toy had matted brown fur and only one remaining button eye.

Joy Chandler clutched the bear to her and answered in the gibberish she still preferred to her limited repertoire of words such as "mama," "dada," "ice cream" and, the one he liked best, "Dabe."

He pushed past Sondra and closed the door before swinging Joy around in his arms. She rewarded him by screeching the coveted word, "Dabe."

"I bet you were coming out to see me. Well, I was coming in to see you." He turned her so she was sitting upright on his hip.

"David, Sondra, can you bring her in here?"

"Just a minute." He released the bundle of energy so he could take his boots off and then followed her padding feet into the family room. Behind him, Sondra hesitated for a second and then followed.

In the comfortable room with overstuffed couches, built-in bookshelves and a TV that wasn't on, Allison rested on a love seat, with a plumped pillow behind her back and an afghan over her knees. Attached to her arm was the long clear tube that connected to the portable IV stand.

"Aren't you thrilled with my surprise?" Allison gestured unnecessarily toward her cousin.

David nodded because his lungs might have exploded if he tried to repeat the word "thrilled."

"Now you said you wanted to apologize to me for your strange behavior last night. And to someone else. I wanted to give you the opportunity." She smiled at him, but she didn't gloat.

Was this how animals caught in live cages felt, trapped inside four walls but with the promise of freedom once it was all over?

He looked back and forth between them and finally began. "Ladies, I'm sorry for being a jerk last night. It was stressful enough without me making it worse."

Allison glanced over at Sondra and then back to him. "Okay, I forgive you, but you probably won't be asked to be Joseph again next year."

David managed to control his temptation to do a happy dance, as it wouldn't make him appear properly contrite. He turned to Sondra.

She spoke before he had the chance. "I'm sorry, too. I wasn't being very nice, either."

"Thanks." He was surprised to realize he wasn't just being polite. Her apology and her acceptance of his gave him a strange relief that he chose not to analyze. "I thought you were trying to leave before the snow came."

"That's the best part," Allison interjected.

David jerked around to face his friend, who looked as excited as a child who'd opened all her presents early.

"Sondra volunteered to stay and to help me over the Christmas holidays. Isn't that great?"

"Great." No one could have missed his lack of enthusiasm, so he rushed to add, "That will be nice for you to have family around." The last sounded authentic because he really wanted it for her.

Allison's grin widened. "It's going to be so much fun spending Joy's first real Christmas—well, one that she's awake for anyway—together." Her eyes filled as she likely remembered last year's Christmas day that she'd spent searching with Brock for Joy's birth mother.

"I'm looking forward to it," Sondra said. "Here, sweetheart, let me help with that." She rushed over to the tree to *help* Joy with the half-dozen ornaments the toddler had already thrown on the floor.

He spoke to Sondra while her back was still turned. "I thought you had to get back to work."

"I don't." She turned back to him, the pillow-type ornaments gathered in her arms. "My office is on shutdown until January third."

"And she's going to stay the whole time." For a woman who'd felt lousy for weeks and was using an IV as an accessory, Allison looked downright giddy. "It will be such a help since Brock's going to have to pull extra holiday shifts at the sheriff's department. It's been tough handling Joy by myself lately."

David sat on the far arm of the love seat and rested his hands on his thighs to keep them from fisting. If she needed help, she could have come to him. Not this cousin who was never around. "Why didn't you say so, kiddo? You know I could have—"

"David William Wright, you've been doing enough for me lately. More than I ever should've let you."

"I haven't done anything. Besides—"

She interrupted him again, this time waving the arm that was free of a tube. "*Besides,* you're busy. The election is coming up. Don't you want to get elected?"

He chuckled at that. "I won't get elected if I work right through Christmas. This is a Christian town, and you know it. No one would appreciate me going door-to-door on Christmas Eve unless I was singing carols, and we both know that wouldn't get me any votes."

She smiled at Sondra conspiratorially. "He's right about that."

She rubbed her chin for a few seconds, appearing to think it over. "Okay, David, you can help if you want. With all I need to finish, I can't afford to turn down any offers. As behind as I am, I'll never catch up."

But Sondra shook her head. "We don't need to put David out. Not when I have the time off. I'm sure if you and I work together, we'll get everything done."

David shook his head just as hard. "She can't help. She needs to rest even if the doctor does agree to take out her IV at this afternoon's appointment."

"Okay, then I'll do it all myself. The list you wrote isn't too long." She glanced at David. "Besides, most of the stuff—decorating, cleaning, wrapping gifts—probably isn't up his alley."

Sondra was doing it again. First, she'd thought she was too good to be set up with him, though he wasn't the slightest bit interested. Now she didn't think he was qualified to do mindless chores. Enough was enough.

"No, I can't promise perfection," he said, pausing to

suggest that someone else was pledging just that, "but I'll do whatever you need."

He gave an exaggerated salute as he turned to Allison. "Your Christmas slave, reporting for duty."

Christmas slave indeed, Sondra thought as she brushed out the house's second and final toilet bowl. A proprietary butler was a better description of David's job title. Every time she started a job, he gave her tips about how her cousin liked things to be done in her house.

"Allison likes her towels tri-folded instead of just in half."

"Allison likes honey in her tea instead of sugar."

"Allison wants Joy to have her nap at one-thirty, not one-fifteen, so she'll wake up later."

Sondra had to admit that he did his share, and he did a good job of cleaning, but if he gave her one more suggestion about what Allison wanted, needed or preferred, she would scream. Besides, he was a guy. How did he even know this stuff about her cousin?

But the answer was simple: time. David had spent far more of it with Allison in the last five years than she had. Her career often had kept her too busy to be with her friends or family, but today it seemed a poor excuse.

She should have been around, especially in the last year when she could have been getting to know Joy. "Dabe" had been there, so the baby loved him instead.

"Are you done with the throne yet?"

Sondra jerked at the sound, hitting her head on the toilet lid. Lifting up, she turned to find him leaning on the doorjamb with his arms crossed. Nothing like adding *in-jury* to *insult*. But as much as her head smarted, she wouldn't give him the satisfaction of seeing her rub it.

"Yes?" She raised an exaggerated eyebrow.

"Oh, sorry about that. I was just going to tell you that I think Allison likes her bathroom—"

She shot out her rubber-gloved hand to interrupt him. "Clean? Yeah, most people do."

Standing up from the commode, she stepped over to the sink and took her time removing the gloves. "I'm finished. I probably haven't done it just the way she likes, but I'm sure Allison will appreciate having a clean house."

Instead of pressing forward with whatever advice he'd been about to give, he nodded. "What does that leave?"

"If you've finished dusting in the living room, then the only room left is the kitchen. But we need to get the rest of those gifts in the closet wrapped before Joy wakes up and has a heyday playing in the bows."

"She'll have plenty of time for that tomorrow."

For the first time all afternoon, they agreed on something. Sondra couldn't wait to spend this special Christmas with the one-year-old, seeing the excitement in those golden brown eyes. It crossed her mind that this might be the closest she ever came to sharing experiences like that with her own children, but she tucked the notion in the back of her mind where it belonged. No sense dwelling on what she didn't have.

"I'll get the packages and meet you in the family

room." Before he could offer any suggestions, she added, "I'll be quiet so I won't wake Allison or Joy."

He nodded and turned the opposite way down the hall. When he was out of sight, Sondra inhaled deeply to calm herself. It was a relief since the air seemed extra thin whenever he was near her.

She found him again in the family room, scissors and cellophane tape already on the floor next to him. With a grunt, she dumped several shopping bags and rolls of wrapping paper on the floor and plopped down next to them.

"You should have let me get all of that."

"I could handle it myself," she shot back.

"I know you could."

She swallowed. "Oh." How was someone who questioned the motives of chivalrous men supposed to take that? Especially when she was tempted to like it. Unable to resist, she glanced at him.

He wasn't laughing. He looked right back at her, not so long as to be called leering but long enough to transform her legs to gelatin. Fortunately, she was already sitting cross-legged on the floor, so she didn't have the humiliation of having her limbs fold under her. Because she was having a hard time breathing again, she turned away and started wrapping a sweet-faced baby doll.

David set to work, too, creating a wrapping paper and tape glob, topped off with a bow. By his second masterpiece, Sondra couldn't help watching him work.

"What?" he asked with an annoyed expression.

"Ever wrapped presents before?"

He shrugged. "Yeah, sure. Hasn't everyone?"

She glanced at his completed pile, and a chuckle bubbled in her throat before she could contain it.

"What are you, the quality inspector?"

"I could have asked you the same question earlier."

He laughed as he attached a long piece of tape over an awkward-shaped package. "Yeah, forget I asked that. How come you get all of the nice square and rectangle boxes while I get all this round stuff?"

"Just lucky, I guess." Swallowing a giggle, she secured a fancy bow on her last package and curled the ribbons with her scissors. When she caught him staring at her package, she explained, "Mom and I compete to have the prettiest wrapped gifts under the tree."

"So that's it. The kinds of gifts you see at my parents' house come professionally wrapped from the jeweler. Mother always pretends she doesn't know where they're from, and we sit around wearing suits and ties and chuckling at her guesses."

"It sounds as if you'll have a blast tomorrow then."

"I will. I'll be here."

"Here?" she repeated, ignoring her racing pulse. The last thing she needed was to spend another day with David.

"You don't think I would miss seeing Joy open her presents tomorrow, do you?"

Her lips pulled up. "Of course not. But your parents live in town. Won't they be upset that you won't be there? Mom is sulking that I won't be in Louisville."

"We'll get together later. They'll barely miss me at dinner since Mother is counting on a meal for twenty-five. It wouldn't be Christmas at Lloyd and Evelyn Wright's home without the mayor, the sheriff, the town board. Mother's serving squab, I hear."

"Does your mother pull off a dinner party like that all by herself?"

"Absolutely." David winked. "Well, she does have the caterer's number on speed dial, and she's careful to set the menu with him by September first."

"Sounds elegant."

"Always."

"And dull."

"Always."

Sondra chuckled. "No wonder you're coming here."

"I can't wait. I'm going to videotape."

He sounded so excited that she couldn't help smiling until another thought struck her. "Wait. You said dinner. I haven't even talked to Allison about what she wants for the Christmas meal."

Panic had her hands sweating. She'd had plenty of titles behind her name, but cook was never one of them. Her only claims to fame in the kitchen were abilities to burn water *and* overcook minute rice.

David waved away her concern with his hand. "Don't worry. It's under control. Allison accepted my offer to make the whole dinner."

She'd just been getting comfortable with him, and here he went again with his one-upmanship best-friend thing. She didn't even know when he would have found time to volunteer to be the holiday chef between completing his own list of chores and critiquing hers. Well, if he'd been confident enough of his cooking skills to offer to do the whole job then they would at least have a decent meal.

At the sound of footsteps, Sondra turned to see Allison padding through the doorway, her IV stand in tow.

"The place looks great, guys."

David crossed to her and placed his hand under her elbow to steady her. "Sweetie, you're supposed to be in bed. If you needed something, you should have called me."

"I'm fine. Really. I need to get cleaned up before my doctor's appointment."

"Uh, okay." He rolled his lips inward, clearly embarrassed that he couldn't help his friend with her personal care, too.

Allison smiled. "Oh, David, I was thinking more about Christmas dinner."

"Don't worry. I've got it all under control. Borkley's Market has a fresh sixteen-pound turkey and yeast rolls waiting for me, and I've got the grocery list ready."

Allison settled back on her sofa daybed. "That's great, but I was thinking—"

"Turkey, sweet potatoes, stuffing, mashed potatoes, rolls, peas, pumpkin pie and chocolate chip cookies for Joy. Can you think of anything else?"

Sondra didn't know about her cousin, but she couldn't think of anything. She was in awe of anyone who could pull a holiday meal together. David apparently could do that with one hand while planning a winning court strategy with the other.

She'd never felt so outdone. He'd finally proven he was a far better choice to help Allison than she could ever hope to be. She should just pack up her bags and give him space to work.

"No, that sounds like a complete menu," Allison said. "But, as I said before I was interrupted, I was thinking that you could use some help in the kitchen. You and Sondra should cook Christmas dinner together. Isn't that a wonderful idea?"

Their answer came as a simultaneous "wonderful" that was as unenthusiastic as David's earlier comment.

David kept staring at Sondra as if expecting her to gracefully decline. *Over my dead body,* a competitive and, this time, dangerous side of her declared. There might be dead bodies, if she did anything more than stir the dinner pot. But the way David was taunting her, she couldn't have backed down now, even for an immediate job promotion. She was in, and she was sticking.

Well, she had about twelve hours to become a cook at least half as incredible as David seemed to think he was. Improbable but not impossible. There was only one thing she knew for sure: This would be a Christmas to remember.

Chapter Four

David closed the door to the wall oven and wiped his hands on his apron. Daylight had barely taken hold on Destiny's Christmas morning, and he and Sondra had already been slaving over a not-yet-hot stove for more than two hours.

Outside the kitchen, the Chandler house was silent as Brock had already left for work and Joy was still snoozing contentedly in her crib. David's gift to Allison this morning would be a few extra hours of shut-eye.

He peeked through the window of the double oven, satisfied to see the dark spices dotting the skin of the still-pink bird.

"Well, that's one thing down."

"One down and ninety-nine to go?"

He turned to see Sondra watching him from the table where she'd been peeling and chopping potatoes and tossing them in a big pot for the last twenty minutes. Already her face was smeared with what looked like flour, and she hadn't even started baking yet.

"You don't have to help, you know," he told her. "It's Christmas morning. Why don't you just relax and let me take care of everything?"

He waited for the sparks to fly since he'd been itching for a fight ever since she'd let him in the front door, looking bright-eyed and fresh-faced.

A not-on-your-life-buddy glare crossed her features before her expression softened to a smile. "I wouldn't dream of deserting you with all of this work, especially on Christmas Day."

Go ahead. Desert me. Make my day. But he managed to contain his version of the famous Clint Eastwood line since he'd only have to apologize for it anyway. He doubted his idea that the only way Sondra could really help him would be to wait outside until she became the ice sculpture wouldn't go over well, either.

"It would be difficult, but I could probably limp along on my own."

"Good thing you won't have to try."

Her smile was a gloating one, so it only annoyed him further that he couldn't help noticing how much prettier she looked when she smiled.

If she thought she was the best "man" for this job just because she could look downright inviting in a frilly apron that said, "Honey the Chef," then she had another think coming. This Christmas dinner was his gig, and he was only letting her play along because it seemed so important to Allison. He hadn't had the heart to tell his friend that it would take a lot more than baking with sugar and vanilla to make her cousin seem sweet to him.

Sondra dropped the last of the potato peels into the garbage and crossed to the sink to wash the potatoes. "So what's next?"

How do I know? What had he been thinking, offering to make the whole meal when he'd never even eaten a homemade Christmas dinner, let alone cooked one? His mother's catering plans didn't sound so bad now.

Why had Allison taken him up on his offer anyway, when she knew perfectly well that his culinary abilities were limited to spaghetti sauce out of a jar and anything with instructions on the box? He shrugged. She probably figured that a Christmas dinner à la canned pasta was better than none at all.

"Why don't you check on Joy while I go over my list?" he asked, to buy some time.

As Sondra left, he released the breath he'd been holding and turned to his notes, which were really only parts of last night's shopping list. Sure, he'd known what to buy from the pictures on the grocery story circular, but beyond that, he was at a loss.

Where exactly did one *stuff* stuffing? How did a candied yam get candied? And what did he do with that can of stuff that looked like cranberry gelatin that he'd already opened by mistake?

What he wouldn't have given if his parents had left him a step-by-step holiday dinner manual under the tree that morning. Still, he would rather let someone *tie* his legs together and bake *him* before he would let Sondra know that someone besides the turkey was winging it here.

"Pie crust," he said when she returned. "Why don't you get started on that?"

Her eyes widened as if he'd just spoken to her in a foreign language, but she squared her shoulders and nodded. "I can do that."

Then she reached into one of the kitchen drawers and pulled out a cookbook.

She answered his questioning glance with a shrug. "Found this last night. Figured it might come in handy."

"Just might." More than she knew. He turned to wash his hands in the sink, trying not to let his relief show.

That he'd been beginning to question their competence suddenly annoyed him. He and Sondra were both college graduates. That meant they had managed to learn a thing or two from books. They could handle this. At least he could.

"Are you making the filling?" she asked as she poured a cup of flour into a mixing bowl.

"Of course." He held up a can of pumpkin that he was pleased to see had a recipe right on the label. He used it as his guide to set the temperature on the lower oven.

"Good. Then it's a team effort."

Well, not exactly a team. More a chef and his kitchen crew. But he decided to keep that to himself, because as much as he hated to admit it, he just might need Sondra's help to get all of this done.

Just as he scraped the pumpkin into a bowl, Allison padded into the kitchen, already dressed in slacks and a loose-fitting blouse instead of her pajamas. She still looked pale, the way she had for the last several weeks, but she was wearing a bright smile.

"Merry Christmas you two. Aren't you guys ready?" she asked as she dragged a hairbrush through her damp hair.

"Happy Christmas, cousin." Sondra waved a flour-covered hand but barely looked up from her mission.

"Merry Christmas. What do you mean, *ready?*" David cocked his head. "Dinner won't be finished for a few hours." How few or how many hours he didn't know for sure, but he didn't want to worry her.

Allison shook her head. "I mean for church. Christmas service. You didn't forget, did you?"

As a matter of fact, he had, and from the way that Sondra jerked her head up from her work, he wasn't alone.

Sondra shrugged. "I usually go Christmas Eve. That's when our church in Louisville has its service. But sure, we can go."

David only frowned. He should have known if he were going to escape the drudgery of his family's picture-perfect Christmas to hang with the Chandlers, it would cost him. The price: church attendance. As if the whole manger event hadn't been a big enough dose of the true Christmas spirit for one year.

This was going to require a different tack. He crossed to Allison and rested his hands on her forearms. "Are you sure you're feeling well enough to go? The doctor said—"

She jerked out of his reach. "I know what he said. That I'm just fine. He even released me from my IV ball and chain."

"Still, he told you to take it easy, to listen to your body…for your sake and for the baby's sake."

Okay, he'd been over the top to mention her unborn child, but he didn't think his action warranted the evil eye she was giving him.

"Of course, you're fine," Sondra interjected in a soothing voice. "He's just concerned about you. We both are."

How did Sondra know *what* he was? And since when did he need a third party intervening for him with his best friend? That answer was simple: since Sondra blew into Destiny. Okay, the evidence was circumstantial, but he was willing to hand down his judgment anyway.

"I'm fine. I don't even feel nauseated this morning. I've missed so much church lately. You're not going to keep me from going on Christmas, are you?"

At the same time, David and Sondra shook their heads. He didn't know what Sondra's excuse was, but he'd already established that he couldn't deny his friend anything.

Allison grinned. "Good. I'll get Joy ready. Can you two be ready in a half hour?"

David shot a glance at Sondra, who lifted an eyebrow before returning to her mixing. Clearly, she was expecting him to answer, to *know* what to answer. He was just going to have to, that was all.

"We'll just toss this pie in the oven and get ready."

Having mixed in the shortening and shaped her flour mess into a ball, Sondra looked up again. "Yeah, it will only take a few minutes."

"Great." Allison rolled her lips inward as if she was holding back a smile as she hurried out of the room.

"She doesn't think we can do this," Sondra said as soon as her cousin was out of earshot.

"Well, she's wrong." Annoyed, he cracked an egg on the side of his bowl and then had to dig a good-sized piece of shell out of the mixture. He frowned at Sondra as she fought back a grin. "Well, she is."

"Okay."

"Is that crust about ready?"

"I guess." Sondra lifted her rolling pin to show him the uneven oval of dough on the counter. "I just have to get it in the pie pan now."

That particular chore required both of them, and some water added to repair the tears in the dough, but before long they had orange-brown filling in the shell and he was settling the creation in the oven. Only a little filling sloshed over the side of the plate and landed on the oven element before he closed the door.

"Well, we did it." Sondra peeked in the oven door and smiled.

"It will be done by the time we get home from church."

They washed up and turned off the kitchen lights. David felt just a little smug with their accomplishment. This Christmas dinner thing was going to be a piece of cake. The best part of all was they would be able to have that cake and eat it, too.

Chapter Five

An acrid scent escaped from the kitchen when Sondra turned Allison's key in the lock and pushed open the side-entrance door.

"The oven!" Sondra shrieked as she rushed into the kitchen. She stared at the oven door, though she couldn't see inside it.

"Aw, man!"

David pressed Joy into her mother's arms, but he must have not heard Allison's helpless "wait" because he rushed over and threw open the lower oven door. A cloud of black smoke rolled upward, and he had to jump back to avoid singeing his eyebrows. Next to him, Sondra shot out of the way, as well.

"Wait," Allison said a second time, and the other two turned to stare.

Balancing a wide-eyed toddler on her hip, she crossed to the back door and propped it open. She turned to face them with a hint of a smile on her lips.

Sondra's reaction was swift and startling. It was all she could do not to throw herself between her cousin and her cooking partner to shield him from criticism. And Allison hadn't even criticized. She'd only smiled when they should have been laughing together. It was funny, wasn't it?

Since when had she and David become allies instead opponents? He certainly hadn't asked for her support, so she couldn't understand her temptation to side with him whether he liked it or not.

As if the situation wasn't chaotic enough, the kitchen smoke alarm started blaring. Sondra grabbed a dishtowel and flapped it below the detector, but the machine continued to squeal.

David pointed to the oven. "You get the pie. I'll get the alarm." He stretched up and pulled the case off the smoke alarm and fiddled with the battery.

While he was still working, Sondra grabbed a pair of oven mitts and reached into the oven. At least she could see inside now well enough to retrieve what was left of the pie. No longer a festive orange, the pastry was charred and oily looking on top, and its crust was so overcooked and brown that parts of it crumbled as she pulled it from the oven. She carried it out the back door and set it on the sidewalk. When it was cool enough not to melt the bag, it would go in the garbage where it belonged.

Behind her, the squawking stopped. David was opening the kitchen window when she came back through the door.

"I don't really like pumpkin pie anyway," she said.

"We torched it just for you." Despite his sardonic tone, David's lips turned up as he said it.

"Wow, my first Christmas present. Thanks."

"You're welcome."

"Was this oven my present?" Allison asked from behind them.

Both turned to see Allison examining her empty oven. Inside it, the liquid filling that had spilled over the sides of the pie had burned all over the heating element and the bottom.

Sondra shook her head. "No, cleaning it will be our present."

"Do you think you could spill something in the garage? Brock needs a present, too."

David curled his lip at her. "I've just crossed you both off my holiday list." He went to her and relieved her of her child. "But this one," he paused to nuzzle the baby, "she can have anything she wants."

Sondra found it sweet the way David stared down at Joy with such adoration, as if he loved her to the bottom of his heart. The man was such a contradiction: someone with a reputed fear of commitment, but clearly his ties to his friends were deeply fused. He was committed. A small part of her wished she could be on the receiving end of David's friendship.

"Hey, Sondra."

She flinched as she realized her cousin had spoken to her. She turned to see Allison studying her. Knowing.

Shaking her head, Sondra tried to cover her slip. "I just can't get over how beautiful Joy is." She approached

Allison and took her hand. "I'm so happy to become a part of her life and to have found my way back into yours."

Allison squeezed her hand, her eyes misting. "Well, you need to know that we're pretty selfish with the people in our lives. I'll have Brock handcuff you and extradite you if you try to slip away again."

"I'll keep that in mind."

Sondra glanced over at David, whose attention was now on the two of them rather than the baby who was playing with the designs in his sweater. To her surprise, he didn't appear jealous of her new relationship with her cousin, but perhaps pleased for her.

"Okay, Allison, it's time for you to lie down so Sondra and I can get Christmas dinner on the table," he said, already returning to his list of details. "It might have to be more simple than we planned, but we should have something together by the time that Brock gets home from his shift."

Sondra nodded. "Sure, we still have a lot of things— turkey, peas, rolls, mashed potatoes. I just have to get the potatoes started."

Moving to the stovetop, she stared into the pan of peeled potatoes. Red and shriveled-looking peeled potatoes.

Her jaw dropped. After several seconds, she finally was able to speak again. "Um…turkey, peas and rolls anyway."

David and Allison crowded up behind her and peered into the pan. When David looked up, he frowned.

"Oh," Allison said before looking up. "They turn colors just like apples if you don't put them in water soon enough after cutting them."

It was Sondra's turn to say "oh." David didn't say anything at all. No condemnation. No *Allison likes her potatoes this way.* He wasn't even laughing. As Sondra kept studying him and expecting him to say something, answers to a few of her questions accumulated in her mind.

Allison cleared her throat. "You know, I am a little tired. Maybe Joy will cuddle up and rest with me until dinner." She reached out her arms for Joy, who went willingly into them. Allison couldn't seem to get out of the room fast enough, and what sounded suspiciously like laughter followed her down the hall.

Sondra waited until her cousin closed her bedroom door before she faced David. "You have no idea what you're doing, do you?"

"What are you talking about?"

"Don't act so innocent with me. You've been dominating the cooking like the next Wolfgang Puck, and you're as clueless in a kitchen as I am. Otherwise, you would have known that potatoes turn red and pumpkin pies can't bake for two-and-a-half hours."

She expected a vehement denial, but David only turned away and dumped the ruined potatoes into the garbage can. When she was certain he wouldn't answer her question, he straightened and met her gaze.

"Guilty."

She shook her head. "Why did you do it?"

He shrugged. "Your guess is as good as mine."

"You wanted to prove to Allison that you could be more valuable to her than some interloping cousin from Kentucky?"

"Okay, your guess is better than mine."

She smiled at that. "Or at least as good. Are you going to let Allison in on your little secret, or am I?"

"She knows."

Sondra stared at him incredulously. "And she was going to let us bang around in the kitchen all day and let me believe you knew what you were doing?"

"As she said, she wasn't in a position to turn down offers. I offered."

I didn't, she wanted to say, but she hadn't exactly refused, either.

David looked in the upper oven at the now golden bird. "At least we'll be able to have a dinner of some kind. The little white thing popped up, so it's supposed to be done. Just pop the peas in the microwave, we'll slice the turkey and, voilà, Christmas dinner."

She stood beside him and peered in. "It looks right, and it smells the way it should, so it's probably okay."

"Sure, it's okay. I always heard that only an idiot could mess up a turkey."

"I would have thought the same thing about potatoes."

He shook his head. "No, never potatoes. Those are hard to make."

She laughed with him then, surprised by both his kindness in letting her off the hook and how good it felt to laugh with him. A voice inside her whispered that she could get used to this, but she tucked it to the back of her mind where it belonged.

"One time I watched a sitcom where the character did something really dumb with a turkey."

He was still laughing. "What did she do?"

"You know that plastic bag thing inside the turkey— the one with the bird's neck, heart, liver and gizzard in it? Well she actually cooked it inside the bird."

David wasn't laughing anymore. In fact, he couldn't have looked more shocked if she'd slapped him.

She stared at him for several seconds. "You didn't!"

He only shoved his hands back through his hair, grumbling things best left unrepeated under his breath.

"You left it inside?"

"I can't believe it. I just can't believe it."

He looked so desolate that she couldn't help feeling sorry for him. She glanced back and forth between David and the turkey that still might have been edible, but there was no way they would be able to serve it. The yuck factor on the entrée would be far too high.

"David, it was just a mistake."

"What are we supposed to feed everyone? Now because of me, there'll be no Christmas dinner."

"Well, they might not have a picture-perfect dinner, but they'll definitely have something to eat."

He met her gaze and lifted a questioning brow.

"You put the peas in the microwave, dump that cranberry sauce in a bowl and put the rolls on the table." She paused until he looked back at her from the microwave. "I'll call for pizza delivery."

Chapter Six

Following the dinner prayer, David lifted his head and opened his eyes. Everyone around him was smiling—Joy, Allison and Sondra. Even Brock had a big grin on his face, probably because he was comfortable out of uniform and dressed in jeans and a sweatshirt.

"'God bless us every one!'" Sondra called out in her best Tiny Tim imitation from *A Christmas Carol*.

Bah. His own traditional Dickens line was on the tip of his tongue again, but he glanced at his friends and took a drink of water instead. They all were his friends now, even Sondra, though it had taken a Christmas dinner of horrors to cement their bond.

He couldn't help smiling at her suggestion that they order out and her determination to find at least one place open on the holiday. Only one had been, but she'd been great—first in not blaming him for the turkey fiasco and then in working with him instead of against him to find a solution. He met Sondra's gaze as he raised his water glass.

"Yes, every one," he said finally.

"I don't know about you guys, but I'm starved," Brock said as he threw open one of the boxes and lifted out a slice of pizza. "It's been a long day—what with booking bank robbers and solving a stack of cold cases."

"Hand out a lot of tickets to families going a little too fast on their way to grandma's house, did you?" David even managed to keep a straight face when he asked it.

The deputy grinned. "Just a lot of warnings. Have to make sure everyone gets there in one piece." Finally, Brock took a bite of the pizza, and his expression was one of pure bliss. "Everything but anchovies. How'd you know that was my favorite kind?"

"How do you know there aren't anchovies on that pizza?" Allison asked her husband nonchalantly as she cut up tiny bites and set them on Joy's high chair tray.

Brock looked suspiciously at the pizza for a few seconds before frowning at her.

"You're safe," Sondra told him. "Your wife promised another round of toilet hugging if we put fish on her pizza."

Though Allison had taken special pains with her makeup and hair to look her best before Brock came home from work, she appeared a little paler than before. The dark circles beneath her eyes were a little more pronounced. She'd been resting for quite a while earlier. Was she sick again?

"Are you okay, pal?" David studied her across the table as he asked.

Allison smiled, but her gaze didn't quite meet his. "I'm fine. Our outing to the services just took more out of me than I expected. I'll probably make it an early night."

"Of course she's fine." Brock grinned. "She's beautiful. But she's got a tough job carrying around our baby while chasing after our big girl. God's got some great plans for this little one."

He touched his wife's abdomen for a few seconds and then lifted her hand. Their fingers laced as if they'd practiced that very gesture daily just to make it appear so effortless now.

David smiled over the love his friends had been so fortunate to find. Suddenly, though, he found himself staring down at Sondra's hand as it rested on the table next to him. The same hand that had gripped his in a firm but cold handshake the night of the nativity performance.

Now he could see that it wasn't a fragile hand. It appeared strong, with fine long fingers and short-trimmed nails. It would probably be warm, too. He wondered how it would feel to fold his fingers around hers and feel them closing over his in a gesture that would be more about sharing than leading or following.

"Hey, good thing these two messed up Christmas dinner. I like pizza better than all that froufrou stuff anyway."

David startled at Brock's words and took a drink of his water to cover his discomfort. What was wrong with him? When had he gone from not liking Sondra at all to definitely not *not* liking her? He was about to damage his reputation as a ladies' man if he let this particular woman get under his skin.

If Sondra noticed his slip, she didn't make any indication, but the hand he'd been regarding slipped gracefully into her lap to grip her napkin. "Hey, Brock, don't accuse us of not being froufrou. We still have Aunt Mary's china and crystal, and a whole batch of chocolate chip cookies that we made with Allison's help."

"I stand corrected then. I just want to compliment the chefs on our great Christmas dinner."

"I'm partial to peanut butter toast myself," Allison replied.

Sondra lifted an eyebrow and looked back and forth between the two of them.

David leaned his head toward her to explain. "That's supposed to be an inside joke about their first date, which really was a makeshift Christmas dinner after they'd been searching all day for Joy's birth mother."

"Remind me never to confide in you again because you can't keep a secret." Allison's attempt at a scowl failed when her lips turned up.

David grinned back at her. "Um, Allison, never tell me anything again because I can't keep a secret."

Sondra straightened in her chair, her slice of pepperoni pizza still dangling in her hand. "I, however, am available should you need a good listening ear that doesn't belong to a blabbermouth."

"I'll keep that in mind," Allison answered, but she looked back and forth between her cousin and friend, as if waiting for the next round of ammunition to be discharged.

David raised both of his hands, palms up. "What? Do you think I'm going to wrestle her to the floor until she cries uncle and says she'll stay away from my friend?"

"It crossed my mind," Allison said in a small voice.

Brock chewed on his pizza, trying not to smile. Sondra looked away, appearing determined not to make eye contact with any of them.

David pressed his lips together but just couldn't keep a straight face. Once he started laughing, he couldn't stop that, either. "Okay, I deserve that."

Sondra raised her hand. "Me, too."

And she started laughing. Brock and Allison followed. Even Joy got in on the action with her high-pitched tinkling laugh, as she clapped her hands in delight.

When he could finally talk again, David turned back to Allison. "So why'd you do it? Or rather why'd you let *us* do it?"

"I already told you, I wasn't in a position to turn down offers as much as I still had to do to get ready for Christmas." She paused to smile at Sondra and David by turns. "You two were competing so hard that this house is cleaner than it's been in a long time."

"Except the oven," Brock chimed.

She nodded. "Except that."

Sondra waved her fork to get a turn. "I'll be cleaning that tomorrow, remember?"

"We," David said simply.

"Right," the other three chimed.

Allison waved her hand. "Anyway, with me out of commission and with Brock out protecting holiday travelers, we couldn't have done all this without you guys. You've made our first Christmas as a family so special."

Brock nodded his agreement. "Yeah, thanks, you two. We really appreciate it. I hated not being here when Allison needed me, but you really came through for us."

They had, hadn't they? But as much as the praise flattered David, it embarrassed him, too. Didn't they realize that even with competing against Sondra, he'd had the best Christmas of his life with them?

The holiday felt different at the Chandler house, as if it was about faith and family, giving and cherishing. If the celebration had touched his heart, just imagine what an impact it would have had on him if he still believed all the lessons he'd been taught in Sunday school.

Disquiet filled him, so David pushed the thoughts away and glanced over at Sondra. She was staring down at the table and twirling her fork in a puddle of pizza sauce and peas on her plate. Clearly, Brock and Allison's praise had affected her, perhaps even humbled her the way it had him.

"Joy sure loved all her toys, especially her baby doll," Sondra said to fill the lull.

Brock laughed. "Not as much as she loved the boxes, the wrapping paper and the bows."

Sondra's head came up, and she quipped, "Even the ones that David wrapped."

"There's nothing wrong with my wrapping ability."

But one side of Allison's mouth popped up, and soon they were all laughing again. Though a fire crackled in the fireplace in the family room, no one in the Chandler house needed it for warmth. It was all around them.

David's chest tightened. He'd always told himself he didn't want or need any of this—a home, a family, something more permanent than the stacked crates of law books and the pressed board dressers in his apartment. But now he wasn't so sure.

Had Sondra changed his mind? No, they barely knew each other. Still, the fact that he was having these thoughts told him he needed to step away and get his head on straight. To sequester himself in a jury room under lock and key. He certainly couldn't do it while Sondra was sitting right there beside him—close enough to touch.

When the snickering finally settled, David pushed away from the table and stood. He stacked several plates to carry into the kitchen.

"Here, let me get those."

Instead of grabbing for her own stack, Sondra reached for the dishes in David's hands. The brush of her fingers over his was unintentional, yet downright electric. David pulled his hand away but not before he shot a glance across the table to see if the sparks had burned anyone else.

Allison had looked away at the right time to miss the exchange, but Brock was staring at him. He lifted a brow.

As if she recognized a tense moment about to become even more strained, Joy spoke up then, her loud babbling filling the room again. As soon as she had all of their attention, the one-year-old reached up her arms and said a brand-new word: "Tonda."

Sondra glanced back over her shoulder as she carried an armload of dishes into the kitchen. Close behind, David balanced heirloom china in one hand and an empty pizza box in the other.

Taking up the rear, Brock carefully carried four water glasses.

"Okay, you guys, just set them on the counter and get out of our kitchen," Brock said. "I'll take care of all this as soon as I get Allison and Joy settled."

Sondra shook her head. "It will only take us a few minutes to get this put away. By the time they're both in bed, we'll be done and you can relax."

Brock set the dishes down and crossed his arms, his legs in the wide stance of a standoff, and the deputy probably wasn't in the habit of losing those.

"You two have done more than your share today. The least I can do is clean up."

David tilted his head at an odd angle and lifted his eyebrow. "Does this mean you're cleaning the oven?"

"Not a chance. You two can take that one on tomorrow. But for now, I want you to vamoose."

David nodded. "Okay. I guess I'll go home then."

"And I'll help Allison get ready for bed," Sondra said. They both started toward the dining room.

"Wait," Brock paused until they stopped. "I was just thinking that there's a really cool Christmas lights display at Hope Park. We'd planned to take Sondra to see it, but since Allison's a little tired, why don't the two of you go together?"

The deer-in-the-headlights look on David's face would have been funny if it hadn't hurt so much. Was being alone with her really such a horrifying idea, especially when Brock's suggestion had sounded like a fine one to her? Too fine for her own good sense.

"It would be great, but I shouldn't. It's getting late, and I need to get home."

Brock cocked his head, seeming to enjoy watching his guest squirm. "Oh, it's not that late. You could walk around the park for an hour and still be at home by ten."

Backing away a step, David tried again. "I still haven't stopped by to exchange gifts with my parents yet."

"Didn't you say your mother would have a houseful of guests and that you could go by tomorrow?"

"Sure, but—"

"I'd really appreciate it. Allison would, too."

David was trapped, and they all knew it. He shrugged and turned to Sondra. "It is a really clear night, so the displays will look great. Want to go see them?"

It was Sondra's turn to be horrified. She couldn't bear the idea of forcing him to escort her. She'd never had to coerce a man into taking her out before, and she wasn't about to start now.

She rolled her lips, too embarrassed to look at him, so she glanced at Brock instead. "You know, I'm kind of tired, too. Maybe I'll just turn in early."

Taking a deep breath, she gathered her courage and faced David. "Thanks so much for the offer, but I think I'll have to—"

She didn't even have the word "decline" formed in her mouth before Brock stepped between them. "You guys are really disappointing me. If you two early-to-bed homebodies are the best examples of quality singles we have around here, then the future for Destiny looks dim."

Instead of responding to Brock, David turned back to Sondra again. "Come on. It will be fun. We can't disappoint the old married folk, can we?"

"Well, with an offer like that, how can I refuse?" And how could she be so pathetic as to have a tripping pulse and sweaty palms over *an offer like that?*

Brock let out an audible sigh. "Good then, that's settled. I didn't think I would ever get the two of you out of my house so I could be alone with my wife."

When both of them jerked their heads to face him, Brock grinned. "Tomorrow's our anniversary, you know."

Sondra was glad this outing would make someone happy because, whether he'd painted on a smile for it or not, David didn't wanted to be with her. But hadn't this whole week been about doing something for her cousin's benefit instead of hers? Her thoughts settled, she grabbed her parka and headed for the door. This would be a night they would probably both remember—as a torture for him and a humiliation for her.

Chapter Seven

Sondra leaned her head back and stared up into the cloudless night sky above Hope Park, awed by the huge black canvas dotted only by a dusting of stars. Though the frigid temperature was a telltale sign that winter had taken up long-term residence in the Hoosier state, the wind wasn't blowing now, so the drifts of powdery snow held their shape rather than constantly transforming.

"It's beautiful, isn't it?" Sondra's question came out as a sigh.

"You mean the lights? They're great."

Under the illumination of the displays and the park safety lights, Sondra could see him clearly, so she was well aware he'd been studying the celestial display rather than the earthbound one just as she had been.

"No. All this." She spread her hands wide and looked up again, inhaling the Christmas air. Her lungs ached over its chill, but she barely noticed. Inside, she felt warmer than she had in days.

"You're right. It's beautiful."

She smiled at his words as they trudged along the park path, the hard-packed base of snow crunching beneath their feet. They passed displays formed of multicolored lights, but these images of Santa Claus and his eight tiny reindeer, Christmas trees and Frosty the Snowman couldn't compare to God's creation displayed above them in twinkling lights.

How ironic that the closest she'd felt to God during the season celebrating Jesus' birth was with David, who Allison had told her was in a "questioning period" about his faith.

"Do you think the shepherds saw a clear sky like this the night Jesus was born?" She swept a hand wide and twirled around to follow it. "Except for the huge star, that is?"

"If I remember the story correctly, in the Book of Luke, it wasn't a star that brought the shepherds to the manger. Wasn't it an angel who showed up in the fields, scared them to death and told them the Good News?"

Sondra chuckled. Speaking of irony, he sure had a good handle on the Scriptures for someone who wasn't sure he believed them. She was reminded of another time when he'd questioned her knowledge on the story of Jesus' birth, but that seemed like a lifetime ago rather than days. A lot could happen in a few days—to perceptions and even to feelings.

"I know. I know." She shook her head. "The only mention of the star in the east came in the Book of Matthew, when the Wise Men were following it. It's strange how we think we know the nativity story, but it has changed so much in the retelling."

He nodded as they passed a particularly large light display with a *Babes in Toyland* theme.

"For instance, if we were being strictly Biblical in the live performance, we wouldn't have had Martin and his fellow Wise Men near the manger since they visited some time later at a house," he said.

"And we wouldn't have had the cows and sheep that the Bible never specifically mentions," she added.

David stood still and looked up at one of the light displays, this one with of a manger scene just like the one they'd performed. He stared at it for several long seconds before turning back to her. "Our donkey-slash-Shetland pony wasn't Scriptural, either, but we liked her anyway."

Sondra couldn't help smiling. She'd expected some awkwardness between them after the way David had been coerced into bringing her, but he'd been really nice.

"Maybe we don't tell the story perfectly, but at least we tell it."

With a nod at her words, David turned back to study the crèche again. Sondra stood admiring it as well, until the wind picked up and sent a chill through her. She pulled her hood tight over her ears.

"If you're cold, we can go."

"No, I'm fine. Allison's boots are great." She caught him glancing at the heavy cold-weather boots. "See Allison and I do have a few things in common. Including really big feet."

"More than a few."

His words brought her head up again, but David looked away before she could study his expression. Were these commonalities good things in his opinion or further reasons to convince him he shouldn't have come tonight?

Neither said anything for several seconds, and when David did speak again, he changed the subject.

"I really didn't want to come here tonight."

"No." The word was out of her mouth, dripping with sarcasm, before she had a chance to censor herself.

The side of his mouth that she could see in profile lifted. At least he thought her outburst was funny instead of pitiful.

"But not for the reasons you must be thinking."

"Which are?"

Both of his shoulders lifted and then dropped. "I don't know. You have to think I didn't want to come here because it was with you."

Sondra had to hold her breath to keep from sighing her relief. As if her sarcastic "no" hadn't been enough of a giveaway.

"I mean, it *was* because I didn't want to go with you, but…"

He let his words fall away just as the nearly inaudible "oh" slipped past her lips. Any lingering hope that he hadn't heard it evaporated when he faced her.

"Look, I'm not saying what I mean here."

He held his hands wide in a plea for understanding, but it was pretty hard to oblige him when she was so busy trying to guard feelings that should never have been this vulnerable in the first place.

"Are you always this eloquent as a speaker in court?"

He chuckled. "Sometimes more so. But let me try, okay?" He didn't wait for her to answer but pressed on as if he couldn't afford to lose momentum. "What I'm saying is I didn't want to come here with you—to be anywhere alone with you—because I wanted…"

What? That she managed not to shout it loudly enough to wake the park's hibernating creatures amazed her. Still, she didn't have to wait long for his answer.

"This." He lifted her gloved hand and laced his leather-clad fingers with hers.

Time must have passed, individual sparkling lights must have blinked on and off a few dozen times in synchronization, but her world paused as she saw nothing but their joined hands. Through his gloves and hers, she could still feel his warmth, and instead of anxiety, his touch brought her peace.

When she glanced up from their hands, David was staring at her. He wasn't laughing or even grinning. If anything, the Casanova of Destiny looked uncertain, and that newest irony of the night made her chuckle.

"If my moves are that funny, then I must be losing my touch."

Somehow she guessed that David had tamed his *moves* on her behalf. She shook her head. "Not funny."

His lips curved up. "Good. I never wanted to be a comedian."

He lifted her hand into the crook of his arm and

started walking again. If this was how wonderful it felt to be a part of a couple, then she wondered why she'd made a habit of keeping her distance.

"From your live nativity performance, I'm guessing you also don't want to be an actor."

"Not if I can help it."

They walked on in a comfortable silence past displays of snowflakes, hammering elves, a trio of Wise Men on camels and a Madonna scene of Mary and the Christ child.

"This isn't your average Christmas lights display, is it?" Sondra said after the last.

"So you noticed. Hope Park is privately owned so there aren't any of those church and state issues. That way many of the displays can show what the owner sees as the true meaning of Christmas."

She couldn't help giving him a sidelong glance to see if he was serious. "What the owner sees? You don't believe Jesus' birth is the true meaning?"

"I used to believe it all." He looked past her to a wooded area. "I don't know what I believe anymore?"

"How could you have played the part if you didn't believe?"

"What can I say? I'm a sap, and my best friend coerced me into doing it."

Sondra glanced at him again. "Didn't it feel dishonest?"

"Sometimes. It did feel a lot like acting."

"But you know the Scriptural nativity story so well."

He glanced up into that clear sky once more. "Knowing and believing aren't the same things."

Sondra stewed on that as they continued on the path. He was right; those things were devastatingly different when it came to eternity. For the first time since he'd taken her hand, she felt cold, but the sensation was inside rather than on her skin's surface, and more for his sake than hers.

"What made you question? I know you were raised in a Christian home. Allison told me your parents go to her church."

"Now there's some acting for you." He looked straight ahead as he walked, his jaw tight. "My parents were too busy being seen in their third-row pew at church and funding events for their high-profile charities to remember they had two boys waiting for them at their so-called Christian home."

"You have a brother?"

"Michael. He's four years older. After college, he bought a ticket to Seattle and never came back."

A lot of things about David were beginning to make sense. "But you did, even if you did join a small law firm known for pro bono work instead of working at the practice your grandfather started in the thirties."

He turned his head to look at her. "How do you know all that?" Then he answered his own question. "Allison."

She made an affirmative sound in her throat. "So part of your protest against your parents is to boycott the faith they taught you."

He appeared to consider it several seconds before answering. "Maybe."

That was likely the closest thing to an admission she

would get, so she didn't push it. Instead, she tilted her head back and studied the patterns of stars above her. "What do you see up in the sky?"

"You mean other than the Big Dipper, Little Dipper and Orion?"

She smiled. "I see God's creation. It's amazing. Maybe it sounds naive, but I really believe He placed those stars up in the sky for us to enjoy."

"Not naive." He stared at those same spots of light.

His words surprised her, but she didn't tell him so. "I have the same kind of feelings about Christ's birth. The live nativity was so poignant to me because it made God's sacrifice real to everyone there."

"The aroma sure was real."

She shook her head at his comment. "Can you imagine the enormity of it? God was sending his son, not to be a little darling asleep on the hay. He was sending Jesus to grow up in the real world and then to die for our sins."

Instead of answering her, he gently pulled away, causing her hand to fall back to her side. He turned to study one of the displays, this one of a choir of angels rejoicing. While he looked, Sondra studied him, trying to ignore how cold her hand felt no longer tucked in the crook of his arm.

"I don't buy it," she said finally.

David glanced over his shoulder in surprise. "Buy what?"

"That you don't believe. You speak of your faith in the past tense, and yet you stare at the stars, just as amazed as I am. I think your faith is still important to you, but maybe you've just lost your way a little."

When he turned back to her, he gave her his endearing half smile. "A little?"

"Okay, maybe a lot, but no matter how far you've traveled, God's always there, waiting for your return."

"It must be comforting to be so certain."

"God's the only certainty I've ever had in my life," she admitted, surprising herself by being so frank. Opening to him felt dangerous in some ways and freeing in others. She didn't know how to reconcile those feelings, and she wasn't prepared to try.

David stepped toward her and took her hand again. "I'm glad you've had your faith to rely on then, because I wouldn't want you to be alone."

Sondra drew in a breath. Just as he'd touched her hand, now he'd caressed her heart. She could almost feel it warming and stretching, opening to him in a way she hadn't expected, hadn't planned. Suddenly, she wanted to touch his heart, too, in a spiritual and a personal way. She didn't want him to be alone, either.

"Are you afraid to let God closer in your life?" she asked him.

His smile was slow, thoughtful, as he rubbed his thumb over the back of her hand. "Sure, I guess. But aren't we all afraid of something?"

Their gazes caught. Held. When he broke the connection, he lowered his gaze to her mouth. He was going to kiss her, and she was going to let him. She felt it with a clarity she'd seldom felt in her life.

But then his words filtered into her thoughts, muddling them. Yes, they both had fears. Her own question came flying backing into her face. Was she afraid? No, she was terrified. Not of her personal relationship with God, but of allowing anyone else to get that close.

Panic had her shoulders tightening, her elbows pressing into her ribs. This was a mistake. Sure, David seemed wonderful now, but what if he were just like her father. He already had a reputation as a scoundrel of sorts. Could she bear to be left again? No, the risk was too great. How would she gather up the pieces of her broken heart when he left?

Unaware of the war inside her, David leaned in so close that she could feel his warm breath on her cheek. Releasing her hand, he instead rested both of his hands on her shoulders. He studied her expression, waited. He was asking for permission. It was so sweet and endearing. But it was also something she couldn't give.

"Uh, David, I can't do this."

Hurt flashed alongside the flickering lights in his eyes before he released her, his expression carefully blank. "Can't or won't?"

She only shook her head. Could she even explain her choices when her heart's survival depended on it? For self-preservation alone, Sondra had pulled back from the only kiss she'd ever truly wanted.

Chapter Eight

That next afternoon David rang the doorbell of the Chandler household for the third time in as many days. Dreading this visit most of all, he wiped some of the new snow off his coat and stomped the gray slush off his boots.

Lord, please let Allison answer the door instead of Sondra. He startled, surprised by how easily he'd re-opened his dialogue with God, particularly when he needed something. And he needed something, all right. He needed to know what to say when he had to face Sondra again.

Unfortunately, he didn't have time to wait for divine inspiration as the woman in question opened the door.

"Hello." Sondra kept glancing up at him from under her lashes, looking as embarrassed as he felt.

"Sorry I'm late. I had breakfast with my parents so we could exchange gifts."

She cocked her head. "What are you doing here?"

"Aren't we supposed to clean the oven?"

"I've already started it. Didn't Allison tell you it's self-cleaning?"

She pressed her lips together, the same lips that he'd come so closing to kissing last night. If he were honest with himself, he would have to admit that he still wanted to kiss her, too, right there on the porch. But admitting it was more than his pride could handle.

By now she was wringing her hands and balancing her weight first on one foot and then the other.

"Are you going to come in out of the cold?"

He grinned. "I guess I could."

Sondra let him in and closed the door behind him, but she seemed to be looking beyond him or beside him. Anywhere but at him.

"I have to get back to the kitchen. Joy's having a snack."

As if on cue, the sound of metal pounding on plastic poured out of the kitchen.

David recognized the sound. "She has her spoon again."

"She loves to beat it on the tray." Sondra led the way into the kitchen where Joy, buckled safely in her high chair, was performing a drum solo with a teaspoon.

Joy paused from beating on the tray and causing Cheerios to bounce to the floor long enough to turn to him and point. "Dabe. Dabe. Dabe."

"Hey there, kiddo," David said.

Sondra bent to pick up some of the mess. "Okay, Joy, we're going to have to eat some of these, too. The ones that haven't hit the floor yet."

David smiled, knowing Sondra couldn't see him and wouldn't ask what he found so amusing. At least they had one safe subject—Joy—in their conversation filled with awkward pauses. He had a pretty good idea that the subjects of their trip to the park and a kiss that didn't happen were off-limits.

Maybe they were better off if they didn't discuss those things anyway. At least it saved him from wondering when he had transformed from a successful social angler to one who could only wonder about the fish who got away.

Even after getting to know him, Sondra apparently still didn't think he was good enough for her. All night the reality of it had eaten at him. But worse than being bothered by it, something inside him made him want to prove her wrong. He wanted to tell her he could be different with her. How could he promise that, though, when even he didn't know whether he would desert her before the never-never land of the third date?

Because that question had no answer and it only exhausted him to search for it, he turned to another safe subject. "Where's Allison?"

"She's resting." She glanced over at him and lowered her voice. "I think she's still recovering from yesterday's excitement."

Concern had him stepping closer to press Sondra for the details he craved. "You're sure she's okay?"

Sondra nodded. "I was worried, too, but she assured me she's just tired."

David felt his body relax. "Well, okay. At least she's taking care of herself."

She smiled at him, the first comfortable expression since he'd arrived. "My cousin is very fortunate to have a friend like you."

"She didn't do so badly in the relative department, either."

"I can't decide if that's praise or not since she didn't exactly choose me." She tilted her head and studied him. "You were talking about *me,* right?"

When she started laughing, David joined in, and Joy giggled and clapped her hands. They were finally over their discomfort from last night, and he didn't want to cause more awkwardness between them, so he decided it would be best for them to just remain friends. Then when she returned to Kentucky, he could wish her well and get back to his own life.

"I'm so glad you talked me into doing this." Sondra spun around on the sidewalk late that afternoon, holding her hands out to catch snowflakes and feeling like a child seeing snow for the first time. "It's beautiful out here."

"I just wanted to get out of the kitchen and away from the smell of the self-cleaning oven burning off the pumpkin pie stuff." He broke into a feigned coughing fit, covering his mouth with one hand and pushing the stroller with the other.

She nodded. "It was pretty bad, but that whole room shone by the time we were finished with it."

"Joy needed to get out of the house for a while, too." He glanced down at the baby, who was asleep and covered with a tiny quilt.

Sondra followed his gaze to the cherublike face. "Looks like she's getting a kick out of the outing."

"The cool air's good for her." He bent to tuck the quilt up to her chin. "We wore her out with all of those swing and slide races."

And they had. They'd built a tiny snowman on the neighborhood school's playground and had shown Joy how to make snow angels, and then David had pushed Sondra on the swing with the child in her lap. They'd even taken a few goofy snapshots on David's digital camera to share with Brock and Allison.

The afternoon would have been perfect if only Sondra could have relaxed and enjoyed it. Instead, she'd spent the whole time watching David with little Joy and wishing for things she'd never dared to before. A husband. Children of her own. She'd always believed those things were only for other women—ones who weren't independent, successful businesswomen like she was. Women who didn't have her particular scars.

Her internal arguments, though, had fallen as flat as the farmland surrounding Destiny. Though an unlikely choice, David was the one who'd made her thoughts about as clear as the mud on those fields. When her feelings for him had metamorphosed from rival to friend to something more, she wasn't sure, but they had changed, and she had to decide what to do about it.

"We should get back to the house," David said as he turned the stroller around. "Allison's probably awake by now and will be getting hungry."

"My hands are getting numb, too."

He glanced down at her gloved hands but didn't say anything. Still, words he hadn't said—that he'd warmed her hand the night before—hung heavily between them.

"You've got snowflakes on your eyelashes." He stopped the stroller, pulled off his glove and reached over to gently brush them away.

Her face tingled where he'd touched her skin, and she didn't seem to have any breath left, so she was surprised she was able to get out a rough "thanks."

"Glad to be of service."

Only when he'd pushed the stroller past could she finally begin to breathe normally again. Just being near him made her feel alive in a way she'd never experienced before, as if she could do anything just because he was near her. But could she overcome her fears? Could she put her trust in any man and open her heart to him completely? Was she made of the right stuff to trust like that?

Even if she could trust, was David a man she could rely on? He could be a good friend; he'd proven that with Allison. But the trail of broken hearts he'd probably left in his wake suggested that friendship was the most she should ask of him. Could she risk asking for more?

The house was dark when they reached it as, lately, dusk had started stealing daylight before the dinner hour.

"Allison forgot to turn on the Christmas lights," David said as they ascended the walk. He parked the stroller beside the porch and took out Allison's keys.

"Maybe she's still sleeping or reading in her room."

He nodded, but he still hurried to unlock the door. "I just want to check in on her. She's been awfully tired all day." As he pushed the door open, he looked back over his shoulder. "Have you got Joy?"

"Yeah." She moved to the stroller and unbuckled the toddler, who immediately awakened with a moan and a stretch. "Go ahead. I'll be right in."

David didn't wait for further encouragement before he rushed into the house, heading straight for Brock and Allison's room. By the time that Sondra had wrestled Joy's snowsuit from the stroller harness and had reached the room with the still bundled child in her arms, David was sitting on the side of the bed. Allison lay on her side under the covers, her knees drawn up to her middle.

Sondra crossed the room in the three long strides. "What is it? What's the matter?"

"I knew it. I just knew something was wrong," David mumbled as he patted his best friend's shoulder. "You've been sick again, haven't you?"

Allison grimaced, her hands pressed against her barely rounded tummy. A soft moan escaped her before she finally forced out the word "cramping."

Sondra blinked. She knew she should do something, but her feet felt rooted to the floor. She should say something, but she didn't have any words. Even with her limited knowledge of pregnancy issues, she knew what cramping signaled: miscarriage. Or maybe something else, equally horrible. After all of Allison's hard work taking care of her body and even after Sondra and

David's battles to be the best care provider to her, she was going to lose her child anyway.

"I paged Brock. Hasn't called back."

"I should have been here," David grumbled again. "I shouldn't have—"

"You've got to stop it, David." Sondra words surprised him as much as they had her. She glanced down at Joy's wide eyes and started swaying so the child didn't cry.

David shook his head, his thoughts appearing to have cleared. "You're right." He turned back to Allison and pushed her hair back from her face as he might have done to a sick child. "We've got to get you to the hospital."

"But Brock—"

"We'll call him. He can meet us at the hospital."

David's clear focus helped Sondra to form a plan of her own. "You get Allison to the car, and I'll see if one of the neighbors can take Joy for a few hours. I'll meet you at the car."

Having a plan helped her keep her thoughts clear as she jogged out the front door with the toddler in her arms. *Lord, please be with Allison and her baby. Hold both of them in the palm of Your hand. Amen.*

Sondra had to knock on three doors before she found someone at home, but Allison's friend down the street offered to keep Joy as long as they needed.

David had her cousin stretched out in the back seat of her car where the infant car seat had been before, and he was waiting in the driver's seat by the time that she came running across the snow-covered lawn to meet them. As soon as she'd climbed in the seat next to Allison and had gathered her close, David threw the gearshift into Reverse.

"Be careful," Sondra told him after he took a fast turn. "You don't want to cause her any more pain."

"I'm doing the best I can, okay?" Without waiting for her answer, he grumbled under his breath, "I should have been there."

Allison's grunt of pain interrupted whatever further self-criticism he would have said next.

"Where's Brock?" Allison murmured.

Sondra squeezed her cousin's arm. "Don't worry, sweetie, he's meeting us there."

"I need him."

"I know you do."

Allison's groan filled the car. "Joy?" she managed.

"She's fine. Jill's watching her."

"The baby…"

At least Allison hadn't phrased the last as a question because Sondra couldn't have answered her if she had. Only God had those answers. Still, she wished there was something she could say to give her cousin hope.

David answered instead. "God's with your baby right now, kiddo. The little one's in good hands."

Sondra tried not to look at him, tried not to lend too much importance to a comment he'd surely made just to comfort his friend. But she couldn't help hoping that David was listening to his own words and that he was aware that God was there to support him, too.

He was going to need the support only God could give. Already, David was holding himself responsible for something over which he had no control. If something happened to Allison or her baby, he would never forgive himself.

Chapter Nine

Just before midnight Sondra leaned back in a stiff vinyl seat at Cox County Hospital, dangling in that void between sleep and wake. But something bumping against her shoulder made her instantly alert.

Next to her, David's head bobbed again and hit her shoulder harder. He woke with a jolt and shot a glance her way. "Sorry."

She smiled. "It's okay. Why don't you just rest for a while?" She patted her shoulder in the silent offer of a temporary resting place.

"Thanks. I'm okay."

It shouldn't have surprised her that David wouldn't allow himself to risk sleep, not when he'd spent the night being strong for everyone else. He hadn't budged from that chair just outside the emergency room entrance since the medical staff had rushed Allison through it. After Brock had arrived to be at his wife's bedside, David had insisted on staying, at least until they were sure his friend would be all right. Even now he stared at the wooden double doors, as if by doing so he could will them open and could wrestle answers from the closed-lipped hospital staff.

Steadfast. That was the best word Sondra could find to describe his actions tonight. She would never be able to think of that word again without being reminded of the last few hours. Without thinking of David Wright.

Strange, she didn't even mind that he'd stayed for Allison's benefit rather than hers. He'd been there for her, too. Strong when she'd felt vulnerable. Solid when her hope had been riddled with holes. The least she could do was offer a brace when his wall of strength wavered.

She reached over and squeezed the hand he'd set on the armrest. This time he accepted her support, which surprised and pleased her.

They were still holding hands when Brock pulled open one of the double doors and approached them, his hair sticking up where he'd been worrying it with his hands. Brock's face appeared as wan and exhausted as Sondra felt.

And then he smiled.

"She's going to be all right." The words spilled from his lips in a rush. "Praise God, she's going…to be fine." Tears that had been close to the surface from his first word trailed down his cheeks unchecked.

Sondra came out of the seat and gathered Brock into her arms. Another question burned in her mind, but how could she ask it? David stood, as well, and squeezed Brock's shoulder.

Finally, Sondra pulled back, but she still gripped Brock's forearms. "The baby?" Her words came out only as a whisper, but Brock stiffened, signaling that he'd heard.

"Oh." He stepped back and shoved his hand through his hair again. "He's just fine. The doctor said it was severe dehydration that caused the cramping. They're pumping his mommy full of liquids right now, and they're going to have to spend the night here, but he's a real trouper."

Sondra was smiling by then and crossed her arms before she answered him. "You mean he or *she,* don't you?"

Brock shook his head and laughed. "After all tests my wife has undergone today, I can tell you that he is a *he.* Joy's going to have a baby brother."

"Congratulations, buddy."

The somber mood of minutes before evaporated as David and Brock were shaking hands and trading pats on the back. Usually, such male antics would have annoyed her, but now she only smiled. *Thank You, Lord, for protecting them.* Then, as an afterthought, she added, *And thank You for sending David...to all of us.*

David returned to the kitchen after transporting Joy from the portable crib at the neighbor's house to her own bed. He would have expected to be relaxed now, to feel exhaustion pooling in his brain like a pothole in a downpour, but he was keyed up instead, his heart and mind racing.

Sondra looked up from the teakettle she was just placing on the stove. "Did she go down easily for you?"

"She grunted a few times, stuck her backside into the air and crashed."

"I doubt it's going to be that easy for me tonight." She indicated the teakettle with a tilt of her head. "I thought some chamomile might help."

"You, too, huh?"

"Would you like to stay and have some?"

"Do you have anything else without caffeine? Chamomile's only for when you're sick, and I'm never *that* sick."

She pointed to the canister on the counter marked "tea" where he found several herb varieties.

"What a night," Sondra said on a sigh when she finally took a seat next to him, her mug in her hand.

"You can say that again."

"What a—"

He raised his hand. "No, don't."

Still, he smiled. Sondra looked as overwhelmed as he felt. He sensed that she understood him, too, and was surprised that the idea of it didn't terrify him. Neither spoke for several minutes, as words felt extraneous to the situation, but finally the need to share filled him.

"I thought I might lose her tonight. My best friend and her baby."

Sondra rested her elbows on the table and steepled her fingers together. "I know." She didn't have to say it aloud for him to know she'd shared his worries and now shared his relief.

"I haven't prayed the way I did tonight in years."

"Me, neither, and I've been going to church all along." She smiled over the rim of her cup. "Did it feel good?"

"Yeah." He pondered that. Even as far as he'd traveled from God the last few years, the Father had still been there with him, giving him comfort he didn't deserve. "I realized a lot of things tonight."

"What do you mean?"

"I relied on Allison a lot more than I knew."

Instead of pressing, Sondra took another sip of her tea, giving him the freedom to elaborate in his own good time. It was as if she understood that he was admitting these truths to himself for the first time, too, and didn't want to rush him.

"If I let my friend fulfill my need for companionship, I didn't have to risk letting anyone else in. To get close. It was easy to change women like I traded dirty socks when I knew that Allison would always be there for me no matter what."

He took a deep breath, as the last was the hardest to admit. "I was lying to myself."

"I'm pretty good at that, too."

He'd been stirring honey into the tea he wasn't really drinking, and his surprise caused him to clink the teaspoon on the porcelain.

"Has Allison told you anything about my father?"

He shook his head. "I'd assumed he died when you were young or something like that."

"Yeah, something like that." The side of her mouth pulled up, but she still looked sad. "He deserted my mother and me when I was seven. Mom gave up her life and her dream of being a professor of literature for this over-the-road trucker who couldn't bear the constraints of marriage, both in its requirement of making a home somewhere and in that pesky fidelity requirement."

The last surprised him, but it also gave him some insight into Sondra's background. He hurt for the betrayal and abandonment she must have felt as a child.

"Mom never really got over any of it," she continued. "She's still bitter, though she did manage to make a home for us by herself and even teaches literature now at the local community college."

He knew of another person who hadn't recovered from the man's collateral damage, but he didn't mention it. "So how does all of that make you a liar?"

"I use my father as an example of why I should never let anyone get close. Plenty of men in this world are just like him."

Not all, he was tempted to say, so he pushed away the thought. "Your theory sounds reasonable." And it did. Hadn't he used his family for the very same purpose?

She took a sip of her tea and set it aside. "You know that teddy bear Joy's been dragging around? It's mine. The last thing Dad ever gave me before he left."

David couldn't stop picturing that poor little girl she probably still was in many ways. A knot lodged in his throat at the thought of that child, clinging to that teddy bear—then and now.

"Where is he now?" he managed when he'd been sure he couldn't speak.

"Letters have come from Chattanooga and Baton

Rouge and even Salt Lake City—usually one every few years or so. But his only true home is the open road."

"You were better off without someone like him. You probably wouldn't be the strong, capable woman you are if he'd stuck around."

"I also wouldn't be the dating nightmare that I am."

They both laughed at that until David finally stopped himself. "You think you're bad. You're talking to a man who's never had a third date with anyone."

She studied him. "Does a third date feel like a marriage proposal or something?"

Surprise had him drawing in a breath. "Something like that."

More like *exactly* like that, but this wasn't the time for specifics. Sondra just *got* him. He wasn't used to women who understood him, except for Allison, who'd always been a friend to him and nothing more.

Sondra shrugged. "I've gotten a few dates beyond three, but not too far past it. I know it's silly, but I figure if I'm always the first to leave, then I'm safe."

"It's not silly."

He understood and, in a lot of ways, had used a similar plan in his own life. His fear was different from hers though. A part of him always wondered if that fear-of-intimacy gene his parents both seemed to carry was hereditary. Until now, it hadn't mattered so much whether he had it in him to really love someone, but Sondra was different than all the others. She tempted him to try.

David didn't realize how quiet he'd become until he glanced at Sondra and found her studying him. An amazed expression shaped her features as though she was just seeing him for the first time, and this time, she'd found him worthy. Funny, he'd never felt less so.

"Your dad really hurt you, didn't he?"

Her only answer was a sad smile.

The rush of emotion came so suddenly and with such intensity that David had to draw in a breath to steady himself. He couldn't stop the words, though, because they came from the heart.

"I would never hurt you."

The need to reach for her was so overwhelming that he had to fist his hands beneath the table to prevent it. He longed to touch her full lips with his, but her refusal from the other night was still fresh in his mind. It had to be her wish that they be together, not just his. So he could do nothing but wait for her to tell him what she wanted.

Sondra drew in an audible breath and chewed her lip. Well, he had his answer, and it wasn't a green light. His disappointment was tinged with other emotions he couldn't define as he gripped the table, preparing to stand.

But the feel of Sondra's fingers covering his stopped him where he sat. "I know" was all she said before she leaned slightly toward him. The trust he saw when he looked into her eyes was his undoing.

Resting his hands on her forearms, he closed the remaining distance between them and pressed his lips to hers. As soon as they touched, he realized his mistake. This was so different from the empty embraces he'd shared with a parade of women. Kissing Sondra felt like an answer to prayer, and he hadn't realized he'd been praying.

He tilted his head and caressed her mouth again, smiling against her skin as her hands traced up his shoulders to his nape. Even after the kiss ended, she didn't pull away but rested her cheek against his.

David closed his eyes, breathing in the sweet scent of wildflowers in her hair. "I could get used to this."

"Me, too," she answered on a sigh.

Because he longed to be a gentleman with her even if he hadn't been one with the women of his past, David came to his feet.

"I'd better get going."

Sondra stood next to him and raised a hand in protest, but he only clasped that hand and drew it to his lips. Then he leaned over and brushed his lips over hers once more. "Good night."

She smiled as he pulled away. "Good night."

Even after David had closed the door behind him and headed out into the frosty night, Sondra remained with him, in his thoughts and in his senses. She'd touched him in a place he'd thought untouchable before—his heart.

Chapter Ten

Just over a month later, Sondra turned off Interstate 69 onto the maze of state roads and county roads leading her back to Destiny. Her chest ached with increasing anticipation as each mile brought her closer to town. Closer to David.

Just outside the town limits, she saw the first of the political signs that made her smile: Be Right—Vote Wright for Superior I Judge. She'd promised David she would make a return visit on his election day, even if she was an out-of-towner and couldn't vote for him. At least the late January weather had cooperated enough to make the journey north from Louisville pretty painless.

"Next time it's your turn to come to my stomping grounds, Mr. Wright," she said to her car's interior. She and David had already agreed as much when he'd first asked her to come the day of the special judicial election. Until now he'd been too busy campaigning to have time for a social life. He had stiff competition in two other local attorneys, both with more legal experience than he had.

More political signs, some for each of the three candidates, dotted the front yards as Sondra reached the center of town. She pulled into the parking lot of New Hope Church, where David had rented the hall for what he hoped would be a victory celebration.

As she climbed out of her car, her gaze went to the open field where their lean-to stable stage had once stood. The stable had still been in place when they'd stopped by during their momentous third real date on New Year's Eve to revisit the location of their unusual first meeting.

What a poignant night that had been, even if David had been more nervous than she'd ever seen him. But then he'd been traveling uncharted waters in his dating experience, so she'd cut him some slack. She'd been ambivalent herself that night, as it was her last evening in town.

She'd also expected that date to be their last.

"Well, look who's rolled out of the big city just to crash the voter polls in Destiny."

The voice that she knew so well from their many phone conversations filtered up behind her, drawing her out of her nostalgia. She turned to see David approaching her.

Trying to ignore her quickening pulse at just the sight of him, she grinned. "I already voted for you three times under three identities. Is that enough?"

He quirked his head. "Just three?"

Instead of waiting for her to come up with another pithy comment, he rushed right up to her, wrapped her in his arms and lifted her, down parka and all, off the ground.

"You're a sight for sore eyes."

"Why, are your eyes sore?"

"No, but my heart sure is."

She blinked over his comment, but she didn't have time to analyze it because as soon as he'd let her feet touch the ground, he covered her mouth with his. The same sweet tremor, the burst of hope and joy that had wrapped itself around her heart the first time they'd kissed, returned with a vengeance. As she had every time she'd thought about it in the last few weeks, she wondered what she'd been afraid of.

After several seconds, she finally caught her breath. "Are you feeling confident about the election results?"

"I am now." He pulled her close enough that they could touch foreheads.

"You mean you were questioning before? I don't believe it." She'd never once questioned whether David would win the election or whether he belonged in Destiny. Her only uncertainties had been over whether, or even how, she would fit into his life.

"No, I've been sure of everything, especially after that great pep talk last night."

"And the night before that and the night before that." She laughed. "Good thing that you had that one-rate long-distance plan."

The fact was they hadn't missed a single night of talking to each other since she'd driven out of Destiny on the first of January, tears streaming down her face and her heart in her hands.

With one hundred and sixty miles between them, it had been easier for her to convince herself that their relationship was simply casual, a friendship really. But now that he was here in the flesh, the lie she'd been telling herself stood out like muddy footprints on a pristine, white carpet.

"Are you cold? We should get inside." Even as he spoke, he flipped up her collar and zipped her coat to her chin. Then he gathered her to him again. "I'm not ready to share you yet."

She closed her eyes and soaked in his warmth, his soap-fresh scent and the comfort of being encircled in his arms. Only after several seconds of bliss did the questions come. Share her? Did that mean he wanted her to be his alone? No, she had to be reading something into his words, was worrying unnecessarily when he hadn't asked her to give up a single thing for him. She was talking about David here. David, who'd dated more women than could crowd into that church hall. But none as many times as he'd been out with her.

Still, they'd had only three real dates that hadn't involved coercion, not nearly enough to constitute a relationship. It didn't matter that she could add to that number twenty-eight daily phone calls, some lasting long into the night. Nor could she let it count that sometimes she felt so connected to him that her arm might have reached out with his hand or her brain might have received messages with his eyes.

They had lives in two different states with careers that mattered to them and people who counted on them. Only someone without a survival instinct wouldn't have recognized that any long-distance relationship between them would be doomed.

They could date as friends and nothing more. She had to be smart. She had to do anything she could think of to keep herself from falling in love with him. But a sinking feeling inside her told her it was already too late.

David glanced around at his cheering friends and political supporters as he stood at the lectern. They wouldn't have to wait long into the night to know the election results after all. Early returns from the three largest voter precincts were so decisive that he could have declared victory an hour before, but he'd delayed out of respect for his worthy opponents.

Nothing could dampen his joy tonight, not even his parents' presence or the fact that his new job would earn them bragging rights with the country club set. He was the new Superior Court judge. He'd even won by a landslide. And if things went his way, the rest of his life would fall neatly into place before the night was over.

He raised his hands to quiet the applause. "Thank you for coming tonight. I appreciate all of you for your support, your friendship and most importantly, for today anyway, your votes."

Getting the laugh he was hoping for, he pressed on, even if his palms were so sweaty that they kept slipping off the wood at the edge of the lectern. "Now that most of the votes are in, the people have spoken, and all I can say is I am privileged and honored to serve as Cox County's newest Superior Court judge."

Brock Chandler popped up on stage then, carrying Joy. Both of them sported "Be Right—Vote Wright" T-shirts, though Joy's covered her to her toes. "Let's hear it for Judge Wright."

The small crowd erupted in cheers and applause that went on for so long that David started to fidget. He'd never been this nervous speaking before, even in front of a judge, prosecutor, a seated jury and a room packed with spectators. But then, though those other speeches had been important to him and critical to a client's freedom, he'd never had so much personally riding on his words.

"Hey, Judge Wright, can you fix my speeding ticket?" a voice on the far side of the room called out.

David jerked his head toward the sound to find Judge Hal Douglas relaxing in one of the room's few arm-chairs with a satisfied grin on his face. The heart attack that had caused him to retire early certainly hadn't taken any of the old codger's spunk.

"Sorry, wrong court—you know that. Besides, I won't be sworn in for three weeks. You'll have to take that one up with Deputy Chandler."

"He gave me the ticket," Hal called out.

"So quit it with the lead foot, Judge," Brock responded.

All of the levity around him only made David more agitated. If he didn't speak up now, the perfect moment he'd planned would have passed him by. It might have taken him a lifetime, but he'd finally found the love he'd always craved. Sondra was everything he could have wanted in a woman and more. All of his life, he had proceeded with caution, always kept up his guard to prevent an uppercut to the chin. But tonight of all nights, he no longer wanted to be cautious. He wanted to tell the world about the woman who'd stolen his heart.

He raised his hands to quiet the crowd again. It took several minutes, but finally the volume lowered a fraction.

"I know you've all been patient, but if you'll humor me just a moment longer, then you can spend the rest of the night enjoying all this good food and great company."

He paused but only long enough to draw his breath and gather his courage. "If any of you haven't met her, I wanted to introduce you to my friend, Sondra Stevens." With a hand, he motioned toward her. "Sondra, could you please come up here?"

Her shoulders stiffened and her eyes went wide before she shook her head slightly and mouthed the word "no."

David only grinned. "Come on, now. Don't be shy." Then he turned back to audience members who were looking at him with odd expressions and beginning to whisper. "Everyone, Sondra needs a little encouragement."

Applause broke out again, until a reluctant Sondra approached the lectern. When she reached him, David stepped down and took her hand. He tilted his head toward her. "This is Sondra. We met over a manger."

A few "Hi, Sondra's" drifted from the crowd before its members became quiet. Expectant. Sondra looked so shocked and uncertain that he longed to take her in his arms and tell her everything would be okay. It was too soon, though. The embrace would come in time, but he had to do this right.

"I have a little something I'd like to say to Sondra, if you all don't mind."

A few chuckles broke the silence as he lowered to one knee. The color had drained from her face. He'd expected laughter from her, maybe even a few tears, but this reaction surprised him. That was okay. He had a lifetime to learn to anticipate her moods and reactions.

"Sondra Stevens, you've made me a changed man. You've shown me how happy my life can be."

She held up her free hand and opened her mouth as if to interrupt him, but he shook his head.

"Please, just let me get this out before I explode." He reached up and clasped her second hand. "I love you, Sondra. I didn't even realize I was capable of that, but it was before I met you."

Her eyes flooded then. Now that was more the reaction he'd expected. It hadn't even hurt to say the words out loud that he'd been hiding for weeks in his heart, so he braced himself for the most important ones he would ever speak.

Releasing her hands, he reached into his suit jacket pocket and produced a tiny felt box. Inside was an emerald-cut solitaire diamond. "I want to build a life with you here in Destiny—to work with you, worship with you, raise children with you. Will you be my wife?"

Sondra lowered her gaze to the ground. Her eyes and her throat burned. She couldn't seem to get enough air to stop the empty ache in her lungs. Tears she'd been fighting from the moment he'd called her up front spilled over her lower lids.

She couldn't look at him or the ring he offered because she might see the hope in his eyes. Then she would be lost. She wouldn't have the strength to deny him, even if it cost her.

"Are you okay?" David asked, perhaps for the first time realizing that all was not well.

She didn't even try to stop the tears anymore as they poured down her cheeks and dripped off her chin. Her chest heaved with the hopelessness that settled around her.

"What is it, Sondra?"

She could hear the concern, the fear in his voice, but she didn't reach out to help him. Couldn't.

David came up from his knee and set the box on the lectern. Though he rested his hands on her shoulders, his touch offered no comfort now.

He probably didn't realize that his offer was just like her father's when he'd asked her mother to let go of her life just to be a part of his. Would David also leave as her father had? Would she be like her mother, alone and bitter?

She was so confused. Her fears crowded in so close about her that she felt smothered by them. David wasn't like her father; she had to believe that. She wouldn't have loved him if he were. Obviously she didn't love him enough though to give up what she wanted for him. He deserved better. Maybe they both did.

Whispers in increasing volume brought her gaze up

from the floor. She only wished they didn't have an audience. Forcing herself, she finally met David's gaze. He was still waiting, though his stark expression showed his hope had deserted him.

"Sondra," he began again, but she raised a hand to stop him.

Each word brought a fresh ache to her heart, but she made herself say them anyway.

"I'm sorry, David. I can't marry you."

Chapter Eleven

David was brooding in his office again that Friday morning. He'd mastered the skill in the last three days since he'd been humiliated in front of most of Destiny. As uncomfortable as he'd often felt about his playboy reputation, it was far worse to know that the whole town knew for certain he was a loser at love.

A call from the law office's administrative assistant saying that he had a guest only annoyed him further. He hated that his pulse tripped at the possibility that Sondra might be the one waiting for him outside. Whether he liked it or not, she'd walked away from him, and she probably wasn't coming back.

Allison was standing outside his office door when he opened it.

"Hey, sweetie." She stood on tiptoe to hug him and then stepped past him into the office. Without asking if he was busy, she lowered herself into the upholstered chair opposite his desk.

"Why don't you have a seat?" he grumbled as he re-turned behind his desk and sat.

"Thanks. I will."

For once, David couldn't muster a smile for his best friend. "What are you doing here?"

"I was just at the obstetrician's." She patted her softly rounded tummy. "I've gained nine whole pounds now."

"That's great."

She nodded, then frowned. "Are you doing okay?"

"Why wouldn't I be?"

"Oh, I don't know. Maybe because Sondra ripped your heart out in front of all your friends and neighbors?"

He brushed his hand through the air and dropped it back on the desk. "Oh, that. It wasn't a big deal."

"Then why did everyone in this office warn me that I was entering a hazardous area by coming in here with you? And why do you look like you haven't slept in a week?"

David shook his head. "I've just been busy getting ready to turn my cases over to the partners before I leave the practice."

"Don't deny that she hurt you, David. Not to me."

He opened his mouth to produce another excuse, but then he clicked it shut. What was the point when his friend could see through him?

"I was wrong about her, that's all."

"Wrong how?"

"To think I could put my trust in her. I know now why I'd never done that before." He shook his head. "I won't make that mistake again."

Allison leaned forward in her chair so that her elbows

touched his desk. "Did you think at all about what you were asking of her?"

"Of course I did." He leaned back and crossed his arms. "I asked her to marry me."

"No, it was more than that. In front of everyone, you asked the woman you said you loved to give up her career, her independence and the life she's made for herself."

"I didn't realize—"

"You knew about her scars, and still you put her on the spot before an audience."

David blinked. She was right. He had known, but it hadn't stopped him from making a fool of both of them. He shook his head at his ignorance.

"Here I was thinking I was making the big gesture, and I was just being a jerk."

"Not a jerk exactly." She paused for a few seconds, as if considering what he'd said, before she spoke again. "But there's something you might want to think about. Love isn't just about having someone to fulfill your need for companionship. It's about being the person that *she* needs. About putting her first."

Having said what she'd intended to, Allison hugged him and left him alone to his brood. Only he couldn't work up the steam anymore. He'd been so selfish. He'd thought only of how loving Sondra could better his life when he should have been worried about how his love could improve hers.

Agape. He remembered the Greek word for God's type of sacrificial love from church, but he'd never before seen how it could apply to his life. He understood now, and he wanted to truly love Sondra, putting her hopes and dreams before his own.

But even love couldn't change the fact that he was tied to Cox County now, and her life was in Kentucky. The distance seemed an insurmountable obstacle between them. Was a compromise even possible, and if it was, then how could he find it?

But the realization struck him that the situation wasn't in his hands. It never had been. *Lord, I know You have all the answers here. If it's Your will for the two of us to be together, I know You'll show us the way. Amen.*

David straightened at his desk, feeling confident for the first time since election night, probably even longer than that. It was a relief from the weight of the embarrassment and resentment he'd been carrying.

The experience of giving up control to God was going to take some getting used to, even if any result had to be better than the mess he'd created all by himself. Still, there had to be something he could do in the meanwhile, instead of simply sitting on his hands. Finally, after all this time, he had an idea that might make a difference.

Of course, God would be in charge from kickoff to the final minute, but the Father probably wouldn't mind if he gave a little help from the sidelines. The idea probably had originated from above, anyway, and he was taking credit for it.

No matter its source, at least his plan gave him something to focus on besides missing Sondra. His energy would have to be divided in three ways, though. The first part would go to prayer, an activity he planned to become an expert in during the next few weeks. The second would go to setting a plan into action. Last, but far from least, he would concentrate on doing something he should have done all along—becoming the kind of man Sondra deserved.

Sondra closed the door to her apartment and flipped on the lights, immediately shrugging out of her suit jacket and kicking off her heels. The flat eggshell walls and neutral décor that she used to find so clean and unencumbered mocked her now, just like the comfort she'd once taken in the anonymity of the city.

Trying to ignore the way the apartment's walls closed in about her, she padded into her bedroom to trade the rest of her work clothes for comfortable sweats. If only she could shake off her malaise inside as easily, because it felt as if nothing could comfort her heart since she'd walked out of David's life.

She didn't have to ask herself how much time had passed since she'd made what might have been the biggest mistake of her life. A clock marking the time elapsed—just two hours short of twenty days now— seemed to have been implanted in her mind. The same way David had imbedded himself in her heart.

As Sondra pulled her favorite Kentucky Wildcats sweatshirt over her head, she wondered what David was doing right then. Did he feel as lonely in his huge warehouse apartment as she did in her tiny flat? No, she would never wish that kind of aloneness on him, or anyone for that matter. She preferred to think of him celebrating tonight with friends before tomorrow's swearing-in ceremony.

Still, when the phone rang, her pulse leaped and again she hoped. Why he would bother calling now, she wasn't even sure. He'd proposed, even if his offer had been unconventional. She was the one who'd said no.

"Hello?" She hoped whoever was on the other end of the line couldn't hear the desperation in her voice.

"Are you finally home from work? Any reason you were there late again?" Jane Stevens never bothered with formal greetings since she spoke to her daughter regularly.

"Hi, Mom. Just paperwork due before that QS 9000 certification inspection."

"It's always something, isn't it? Are you okay?"

Her answer was automatic and at least as honest as Sondra had been with herself lately. "Yeah, I'm fine."

She held her breath, hoping they could drop the subject this time. Discussing her broken heart with her mother just didn't feel right. Sure, Jane could relate, but her bitterness felt toxic. *You see, men are all the same.* Her mother's words still rang in Sondra's ears, yet they didn't ring true. David wasn't the same. He couldn't be.

Her mother made a scoffing sound into the phone, and Sondra braced herself.

"Honey, you're not fine. You're not fine at all."

She couldn't listen to it, couldn't bear to hear "I told you so" again. "Mom—"

"And it's all my fault," Jane continued.

Sondra started. "What…what are you saying?"

"I was wrong." An audible sigh came through the phone line. "I was hurt, but I've hurt you most of all."

"No, Mom, it was Dad. He hurt us."

"Sweetheart, listen to me. You can't base decisions about your life on our mistakes—your father's and mine."

Sondra was tempted to argue, to defend her mother's honor, but something stopped her. Maybe her mother was ready to let some of her anger go.

"Marriage is about giving and taking, about loving even on days when your spouse is unlovable. If only I had trusted God with the situation, things might have been different."

Sondra had to disagree this time. "You can't hold yourself responsible for his desertion, his infidelity."

"I couldn't forgive. I taught my own daughter not to trust people. I became a bitter, lonely woman."

"You loved me, Mom. You raised me the best you could, all by yourself."

Again Jane's breathing was audible. Resigned. "Do you love him, Sondra?"

She didn't even hesitate. "Yes. I love him."

"Then don't close the door so easily. Don't be alone…like me."

Jane said nothing for several seconds, and when she did speak, her voice sounded gravelly, as if she were crying. In all her life, Sondra had never seen her mother cry, even in the days after her father had left. Jane had only remained stoic and icy cold.

"Please, please put the situation in God's hands," Jane told her.

Sondra barely heard the other things her mother said before Jane ended the call. As if her thoughts hadn't been muddled enough since the election-night fiasco when she'd rushed back to Louisville and tried to bury her hurt in her work.

She couldn't imagine a more unlikely source for relationship advice, but her mother was there giving it. That was only one of the contradictions she was beginning to recognize in her life. Another was her career. Had power in the corporate world ever really been her dream, or had her career only been a safe haven from real world personal relationships? She wasn't sure.

And did she even want to *have it all* in terms of job titles and prestige and to *have nothing* when she returned home at night?

Sondra didn't have to ask herself that question twice. No, she didn't want that. She wanted a life that was filled with smiles and laughter, with faith and love. And she wanted all those things with David.

Before she realized what she was doing, she was throwing clothes and cosmetics in a bag. She would have to call into work from the road, but that wouldn't be a problem since she had plenty of flextime available from all her overtime work lately.

She wasn't sure what would happen when she reached Indiana or even whether David had changed his mind about her. He hadn't called, but then neither had she. Still, she had to go, had to follow God's urging and her heart. For her, it seemed that all roads led back to David and to her Destiny.

Chapter Twelve

The next morning David stood with his right hand raised and his left hand on a Bible as he was sworn in as the new judge for Cox County Superior Court I. David shifted in his long black robe, feeling uncomfortable in the garment. It would grow on him and he would grow into the role it represented in the coming months.

The courtroom looked different somehow, though he'd spent plenty of hours on the other side of that gleaming mahogany desk where he would now preside. The twin desks where the prosecution and the defense made their cases appeared smaller than he remembered.

Judge Douglas leaned on a cane as he swore in his replacement. "I would like to present the Honorable David William Wright."

The sound of applause around him only added to the surreal feeling that came with achieving a goal of being judge two years before his thirtieth birthday. Several of his supporters had taken time out from their busy lives to share his achievement with him. Allison waved when she caught his attention. She and Brock stood next to David's parents. David could pick out fellow defense attorneys, friends from the prosecutor's office and even Martin Rich from the live nativity among the guests.

Only one person was conspicuously absent, but he shouldn't have expected Sondra to show. After his too-public proposal and her humbling refusal, she would probably feel too conspicuous anyway. He hadn't realized how much he'd still hoped, until disappointment filtered through him. Maybe he was just as mistaken in believing there was a chance for them at all.

And then someone pulled the courtroom door open and there she was.

David's breath caught in his throat. It seemed as if it took forever to reach her as he wound his way through the crowd, shaking a few hands as he passed, but finally they came face-to-face.

"Hey."

"Hi." She still wore her parka and a stocking cap, and both were wet with snow. "Um…sorry I'm late."

"I'm glad you came. Thanks." David kept his hands to his sides instead of reaching out to grip hers. He'd never in his life wanted to touch another human being more than he wanted to gather her into his arms right then, but he wasn't entirely sure he'd be able to let her go.

"The drive was rough."

"You just drove up this morning?"

"Well, I started last night, but it was slow trip on Interstate 65 with the snow blowing."

David swallowed. "You shouldn't have taken that kind of risk just to be here for this." He didn't know what he would have done if she'd been in an accident while making her way north to the event. To him.

"I really wanted to be here for this."

He lifted an eyebrow, still not certain what statement she'd made by coming. "Then I'm glad you made it in one piece."

Sondra was looking about nervously as if she'd noticed that they had a crowd. It shouldn't have surprised her after their very public last meeting. He was sorry about that. He was sorry about a lot of things. Because having an audience had been a mistake last time, and he didn't want to repeat it, he took her by the arm and ushered her into his new judge's chambers.

"Sondra, I—"

"David, I—"

Because they both began at the same time and in the same way, they laughed, but the sound died away quickly.

"Really, Sondra, let me—"

She shook her head to stop him. "You have to give me the chance—"

"No, I need you to understand that I didn't mean to embarrass—"

"Please, David. Let me say I'm sorry."

The side of his mouth pulled up despite his best effort to remain serious. Only the two of them were competitive enough to battle about anything, even being the first to apologize.

"Okay, you win." David indicated with his hand for her to take one of the guest chairs opposite his new desk, and he sat in the other. "You go first, but you don't have anything to be sorry about."

Sondra pressed her lips together, and her eyes shone too brightly. After several seconds, she finally spoke. "I'm so sorry about what happened the night of the election. Your question just took me by surprise."

"Hit you broadside is more like it."

"That, too." She shrugged. "I was surprised and terrified and…just not ready. All I could think about was what I would be giving up. Not what I would gain."

Gain? He studied her face, looking for hidden meanings in her words. Had she found his offer worth considering, even before, when it was so one-sided? Even though he knew it was risky, he still was tempted to hope.

His words came out in a rush. "I shouldn't have asked in front of everyone. I didn't even realize what I'd asked you to sacrifice. I shouldn't have expected you to give up your whole life for me. I had no right."

Though her eyes were still shiny, a smile appeared on her lips. "I thought you said I could go first."

He held his hands wide and opened his mouth to explain but then closed it again. "Okay, go ahead."

She nodded but didn't speak right away. Her smile vanished, and she chewed her lip. His stomach tightened as his already tenuous hope wavered, but still he waited.

Sondra's heart beat so furiously in her chest that she was convinced David could hear it. Her eyes burned with the emotion dwelling so close to the surface. How could she tell him what was in her heart? Could she lay herself bare that way? What if— No, she wouldn't allow her fears to keep her from having what she needed. Not this time.

Taking a deep breath, she began. "I'm sorry I humiliated you in front of, well, everyone. I was scared. I'm still scared."

Strange, as she spoke the words aloud, her feelings inside contradicted her. She didn't feel frightened anymore. Inside her was this strange calm assurance that all would be well. "I didn't know if I was ready to give up my plans, my dreams, for anyone."

He leaned forward in his chair. "You see, you don't have to—"

"David, are you going to let me finish this here, or will I have to go deliver it as a speech from the judge's seat where you won't interrupt?"

He closed his mouth and waved with his hand for her to proceed, but from his expression, it appeared that whatever he had to say was making him crazy. She could relate to that, yet she had to slow her thoughts if she wanted to do this right. And she wanted that in the worst way.

"What I didn't realize was that since I'd met you, my dreams had changed. I didn't want the same things anymore. So I wouldn't have to give up anything to have everything I wanted."

David opened his mouth, preparing to interrupt her again, but he must have remembered because he shook his head and stopped himself.

Sondra only smiled. Always the courtroom attorney, David would forever try to get the last word in during their unavoidable debates, but she looked forward to their disagreements and to the opportunity to make up after them.

"What I want, David, is you. I'm in love with you, and I want to build a life with you right here in Destiny. That is, if the offer still stands."

Facing her, David leaned so close that she could see every facet of his translucent blue eyes and could feel his warm breath on her cheek. Her hands were already trembling before he reached for them. As their fingers laced, Sondra felt a tremor that made her wonder if hers were the only hands that had been shaking.

But then the side of David's mouth lifted. "Now you're all done apologizing, right? Because I wouldn't want to develop a reputation as a man who can't take turns."

The emotion that had been clogging her throat dislodged in a nervous giggle. "I'm all done."

"Sure?" At her nod, he smiled. "Okay, now, what was I apologizing for? Oh wait, I remember. I'm sorry I proposed to you in front of everyone in town."

He paused, his expression becoming serious as he peered so deeply into her eyes that he must have been able to see into her heart as well.

"But my proposal was real. The offer, flawed as it is, will be there whenever you're ready to accept it. You're the only woman I've ever loved or will ever love. I know it's God's plan for us to be together, so I'll be waiting until you're ready."

Sondra wasn't sure whether she had moved her head first or if David had shifted, but suddenly his lips were touching hers, sealing those promises with his kiss. She folded her arms behind his neck, feeling strength in acquiescence, freedom in entrusting him with her heart.

When David pulled away, he was wearing one of his mischievous smiles. "Are you prepared to hear my proposal again? I've just added an element that I'm sure you'll find will really sweeten the deal."

Sondra shook her head, and, in case he hadn't gotten the message, she said it aloud. "No."

He rested his hands on her forearms, and his grip tightened reflexively. "What do you mean? No, you don't want to hear my proposal again? Or are you saying 'no' to my proposal?"

She blew out a breath, amazed that after all she'd told him, he could still worry that she would shoot him down.

"Neither. I don't need to hear the proposal again, though I would probably enjoy hearing those words in private instead of over a public address system. And, no, I don't need you to sweeten the offer. The only thing I need is you."

David just looked at her for so long with his eyebrows drawn together in confusion that she took pity on him.

She cleared her throat. "Are you going to ask me again, or aren't you?"

"Well, when you put it like that…." He let his words trail off, but he still slipped out of his chair, black robe and all, and came to rest on one knee in front of her.

Déjà vu had her drawing in a sharp breath, but the man she loved only continued to smile. That smile was so appealing that she couldn't help returning it.

"Sondra, if you agree to be my wife, I'll spend every day making sure you know you made the right decision." He took a deep breath. "Will you marry me?"

The word "yes" had barely crossed her lips before he lifted up to press his mouth to hers. His arms came around her in a fierce hug, and then his lips caressed hers again in a kiss of hope, of permanence. Moving back from her, he stood and crossed to the corner of his office where his suit jacket hung on a coat tree. He reached in the pocket and produced a felt box Sondra recognized.

He pointed to the box and raised an eyebrow, and at her nod, opened it. The emerald-cut diamond ring was still nestled inside it. David returned and crouched in front of her, finally lifting out the ring and slipping it on her finger where it belonged.

Sondra stared down at her hand, as amazed by the promise the ring represented as by its glimmering beauty. But then she lifted her head to look up at him again. "You had the ring with you. How did you know I'd be here?"

"I didn't. I was only hoping. If you hadn't come today, I was planning a road trip to Louisville."

She feigned a shocked look. "You mean I could have saved myself a treacherous journey on icy Indiana roads if I'd only waited a few days?"

"Guess so." He stood up and pulled her with him, gathering her into his arms once more. "I also guess we have some news to share with the crowd out there." He indicated the door with a tilt of his head.

"Wouldn't they have all gone back to their own busy lives by now?"

David rolled his eyes. "With the two of us in here? Are you kidding? I guess I'll have to teach you a thing or two about life in a small town."

"So I take it we're big news?"

"The newspaper photographer should be arriving at any minute."

Chapter Thirteen

As it turned out, the photographer was already waiting when they came out of the door. And just as David had predicted, most of the ceremony guests were still milling around, munching on the light snacks and waiting for news.

David grinned at his new fiancée's shocked expression. He supposed he could have told her that the *Destiny Post* photographer was just late showing up for his swearing-in ceremony, but he enjoyed seeing her surprise.

He hoped his announcement would shock her just as much and please her a whole lot more. No doubt the *Post* photographer, who'd been at the paper since Lyndon Johnson was president, would be happy he'd been tardy, too, since he would get to break the story that would eventually make statewide news.

"May I have everyone's attention please," David said needlessly, since the room was already becoming quiet as he crossed to the lectern where defense and prosecution usually made their cases.

He gestured for Sondra to come nearer, and her shoulders tightened at the repeat of the earlier fiasco, but she came to him and took the hand he offered. "I wanted to announce to you all that the population of Destiny, Indiana, is about to become seven hundred and one. I have asked Sondra Stevens, the love of my life, to marry me—again—and she has agreed."

A whoop that could only have been from Brock Chandler rose up from the crowd.

"You sure she said yes this time?" Judge Douglas called out from the chair where he was resting.

"I'm sure." He lifted the hand he held, which happened to be the one on which she wore his ring.

"What'd ya have to promise her?" Hal Douglas prodded.

"That I'd be an incredible husband." In effect, he had said that, and he was determined to keep that promise. "I even offered to sweeten the deal to convince her to stay here with me in Destiny, but Sondra wouldn't hear of it. I'm thanking God for my blessings because she agreed to marry me without any perks.

"That makes my gift to her and to the community that much more special." Unable to resist, David pulled Sondra to him and kissed her, right there in front of his parents and everyone.

Sondra waved her hand in front of her face, clearly embarrassed, but she was smiling, too. He watched her until she drew her eyebrows together in a questioning expression.

"Spill it, Wright, or we'll be here until next Christmas," Brock called out.

He waved at the deputy, who held little Joy in his arms. "I didn't think it was fair to make my wife-to-be give up her life to come to Destiny, but I also couldn't move Cox County Courts across the state line. A compromise was to bring at least part of Sondra's work with her."

David glanced once more at Sondra's perplexed expression before his big announcement.

"With a little help from that trust fund from my grandparents that was languishing at First National, I have purchased the site of the now-defunct Clear View Motel and surrounding properties. On that site, if my fiancée agrees to it anyway, I hope to build the largest recreational vehicle dealership and parts and service center in east-central Indiana."

Because Sondra appeared more shell-shocked than thrilled as she stared into the crowd, David rushed on anxiously. Why did he insist on continuing to surprise her in public? He was still a member of the group that never learned from its mistakes—just him and that three-legged dog. But he was ready to burn his membership card.

He spoke to the crowd but watched her in his peripheral vision, hoping to see her eyes light up, or a smile or anything to suggest that his idea wasn't a big mistake.

"A combination facility like this could provide job

opportunities for Destiny residents as well as bring tourism dollars to Cox County. There might even be a possibility for an RV park near Clemens Reservoir…."

His words trailed off as he caught sight of Sondra staring at him now, her expression incredulous. "Are you kidding?" Her words were just above a whisper.

He continued, this time meeting her gaze. "But all of that would be up to the dealership's owner and operator: Sondra Stevens—soon to be Wright."

She shook her head. "You can't be serious."

"I am." But her comment made him second-guess whether he should be.

Whatever she'd been about to say after that was drowned out by applause that flooded the room. Everyone around them recognized that the idea would benefit Destiny. The court was still out on whether it would be a good thing for the woman he loved.

"If you get the approvals, do you have a name in mind for the place?" the photographer called from the rear of the room.

He shook his head. "Not at all. That and the rest of the decisions would be up to the owner/operator."

"How about Clear Rolling?" Judge Douglas supplied.

"I know," Allison called out. "Clear Roads Ahead."

Soon names were being bandied about over a business that was still no more than a pipe dream. Only Sondra hadn't contributed, hadn't said anything more.

David backpedaled as quickly as he could. "All of this is very preliminary. We won't go forward with it at all if it's not what's best for Sondra."

"We'll call it the Road to Destiny RV Center."

He turned at the sound of her voice, and she was smiling back at him. "You did this for me?" she whispered.

Then she turned back to the crowd of people who had supported him and would accept and support her just the same. "Does anybody here wonder why I'm in love with this guy?"

After several few minutes and a lot more excited ramblings about the proposed dealership, the crowd began to dissipate. As soon as they were alone in the courtroom, David led Sondra back to his chambers. He removed the judge's robe from over his shirt and tie and hung it on the coat tree.

He was only halfway into his suit jacket before Sondra threw herself into his arms. She pressed her lips to his and pulled back, still resting her hands on his shoulders.

"I still can't believe you did all of this for me. Where did you even get the idea?"

"It started with Allison giving a lecture about what real love was. God put His two cents in, as well, and I listened."

"Looks like you mastered the skill."

Tilting his head, he lowered his mouth to hers and kissed her with all the hopes, dreams and promises in his heart. So this was what it felt like to have everything he'd ever wanted in life—even the parts he'd never realized he could ask for.

When he pulled away, he rested his forehead against hers. "Loving you is the best thing I've ever done. I'm determined to do it well for the rest of our lives."

She smiled back at him. "Don't worry, I'll be here to see that you do."

On a snowy Sunday afternoon in early March, Sondra processed down the aisle of New Hope Church toward the man who had earned her heart. His eyes were shining with tears as she approached him in her simple white gown. She had to blink back tears of her own when he smiled at her.

"You're so beautiful," he said, not bothering to whisper.

"You're pretty handsome yourself."

Until she heard the chuckles behind her, Sondra had almost forgotten they weren't alone in the sanctuary. Still, the ceremony was private, just the way she wanted it. She insisted that it had been enough that they'd met in a stable stage, and he'd proposed during an acceptance speech.

As she glanced back at their few guests—the Chandlers, her mother and his parents—she was convinced she'd made the right decision.

When she turned back to him, David held out his hand. Without hesitation, she placed her hand in his, just as she was entrusting him with her heart and her future. *Thank You, Father, for sending David to me.*

"Do you take this man to be your lawfully wedded husband?" Reverend Jeff Reed asked.

"I will."

The words she'd never expected to say came so easily. She wasn't afraid, and she knew she never needed to fear while in the security of David's arms. His love was steadfast and sure.

"David, will you love, honor and keep her, forsaking all others, keep you only to her, as long as you both shall live?"

"You bet I will," David answered to laughter from their audience.

Soon the formalities were over, and David drew her into his arms.

"This is for forever," he whispered as he lowered his head for their first kiss as husband and wife.

Bliss. That was the only way she could describe feelings welling inside her as he took her hand and led her up the aisle.

They'd come so far to reach this point, these vows, and a faith they could share in a life together. It felt as if they'd run a marathon coming from opposite directions to the same finish line. Only the race didn't end here. It was only the beginning. From this point on, they would run side by side.

* * * * *

Dear Reader,

My friend Irene Brand and I wish you joy this Christmas season as we celebrate God's great gift to a dark world in the form of His son, Jesus. For the two of us, writing *Christmas in the Air* has been like a warm holiday visit with old friends. In our novellas, we have revisited characters from our earlier stories in *A Family for Christmas,* sharing with them as they open their hearts to the peace of the Christ Child.

In my novella, "A Season of Hope," the characters learn about the perfection of God's plan and His timing, even in the unlikely location of a stable stage. Ladies' man David Wright must finally face his fear of commitment during a face-off with independent businesswoman Sondra Stevens, who harbors her own emotional scars. Can they open their hearts to love's possibilities without receiving more visible wounds? Anything's possible in this season of hope.

Dana Corbit

Love Inspired®

TITLES AVAILABLE NEXT MONTH

Don't miss these four stories in November

LOVING TENDERNESS by Gail Gaymer Martin
Part of the LOVING miniseries

After her car broke down, Hannah Currey was relieved when caring stranger Andrew Somerville helped her find refuge. His gentle attention helped her believe in love again. But with a painful secret haunting her, would Hannah be able to return the love this one-in-a-million man so deserved?

HER CHRISTMAS WISH by Kathryn Springer
Tiny Blessings

Little Olivia wants a new mommy for Christmas, and she's got just the person picked out. Who could be more perfect than her new nanny, Leah? After all, her widowed father's been smiling more since Leah started. Will Olivia get her Christmas wish?

JOY IN HIS HEART by Kate Welsh

Joy Fuller knew she couldn't marry Brian Peterson. He wanted a society wife, not a tomboyish pilot. That's what Joy told herself when they broke up. Now, twelve years later, they're thrown together on a rescue mission. And if they can stop quarreling, they might realize they're still hopelessly in love.

IN THE SPIRIT OF...CHRISTMAS by Linda Goodnight

As December approached, Christmas tree farm owner Lindsey Mitchell desperately needed assistance. She hired widower Jesse Slater, who fit right in...except when it came to holiday spirit. Can Lindsey teach him and his adorable daughter the true meaning of Christmas?

LICNM1005